HOW TO DRAW
CARTOONS, MO   5
ANIMALS & MACHINES

Part One
HOW TO DRAW CARTOONS AND CARICATURES
Judy Tatchell

Designed by Graham Round

Illustrated by Graham Round, Terry Bave, Robert Walster and Chris Lyon

Additional designs by Brian Robertson and Camilla Luff

Contents

Consultants: Terry and Shiela Bave

NORTH LEAMINGTON SCHOOL

About part one

Caricature

The first part of this book is all about how to draw cartoons. It is full of simple methods you can use and lots of pictures to copy and give you ideas.

The next few pages tell you how to draw cartoon people using simple shapes and lines. You can find out how to draw movement and expressions, too.

A caricature is a funny picture of a real person. You exaggerate things, such as the shape of their nose or hair. You can find out how to do this on pages 8-9.

A cartoon story book.

YAP!

A strip cartoon is a series of pictures which tell a joke or funny short story. You can find out how to build up your own strip cartoons on pages 24-25.

Looking at a cartoon story book is a bit like watching a film and reading a book at the same time. You can see how the Tintin stories were created on pages 30-31.

On pages 34-37, you can find out how cartoon films are made. This is called animation, which means "the giving of life". Cartoons are brought to life in a film.

First faces

This page shows you an easy way to draw cartoon faces. All you need is a pencil and a sheet of paper. If you want to colour the faces in, you can use crayons or felt tips.

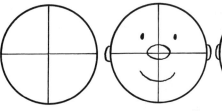

Draw a circle. Do two pencil lines crossing it. Put the nose where the lines cross. The ears are level with the nose. The eyes go slightly above the nose. Rub out the lines crossing the face. Add any sort of hair you like.

Faces to copy

Here are some more faces for you to copy. You can see how in a cartoon some things are exaggerated, such as the size of the nose or the expression.

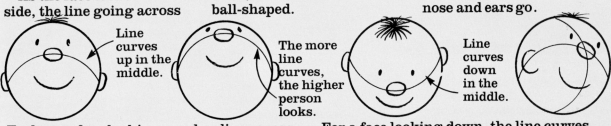

Looking around

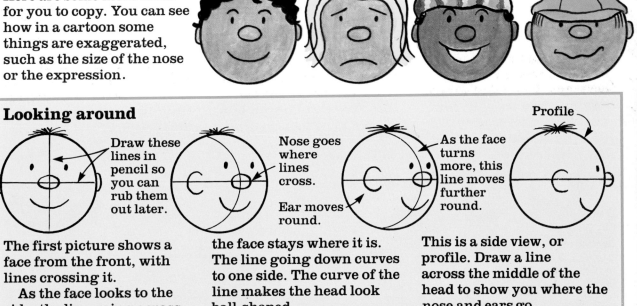

Draw these lines in pencil so you can rub them out later.

Nose goes where lines cross.

Ear moves round.

As the face turns more, this line moves further round.

Profile

The first picture shows a face from the front, with lines crossing it.

As the face looks to the side, the line going across the face stays where it is. The line going down curves to one side. The curve of the line makes the head look ball-shaped.

This is a side view, or profile. Draw a line across the middle of the head to show you where the nose and ears go.

Line curves up in the middle.

The more line curves, the higher person looks.

Line curves down in the middle.

To draw a face looking up, do a line across the face as shown. The nose goes in the centre and the ears at each end of the line.

For a face looking down, the line curves down in the middle. Can you see how the face looking up and to one side is drawn?

3

Cartoon people

Now you can try adding some bodies to your cartoon faces. There are two different methods described on these pages. The first uses stick figures. The second uses rounded shapes. Try them both and see which you find easier.

Stick figures

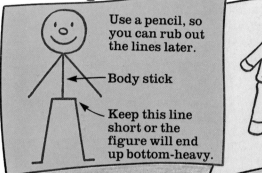

Use a pencil, so you can rub out the lines later.

Body stick

Keep this line short or the figure will end up bottom-heavy.

Rub out a bit of the head line here, where the hair falls forward.

Draw this stick figure. The body stick is slightly longer than the head. The legs are slightly longer than the body. The arms are a little shorter than the legs.

Here are the outlines of some clothes for the figure. You can copy a sweatshirt with jeans or with a skirt. You could also try some dungarees or a dress.

To dress your stick figure, draw the clothes round it, starting at the neck and working down.

You can add long, short, curly or straight hair.

Drawing hands and feet

When someone is facing you, you can see their thumbs and first fingers.

People's feet usually turn out a bit.

Cartoon hands and shoes, like cartoon heads, are larger than on a real person. Practise drawing these shapes before you add them to the figures.

Colouring in

Use a fine felt tip pen for the outline.

A cartoon person's head is larger than on a real person.

Give her socks if you like.

Shiny white patch on shoes.

When you have finished the outline of the figure, go over it with a felt tip pen. When it is dry you can rub out the stick figure and colour the cartoon in.

The girl needs some lines for legs before you can put on her shoes. When you colour the shoes, leave a small, white patch on the toes to make them shiny.

Figures using rounded shapes

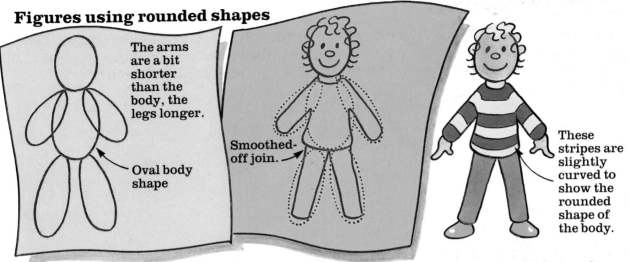

The arms are a bit shorter than the body, the legs longer.

Oval body shape

Smoothed-off join.

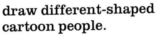

These stripes are slightly curved to show the rounded shape of the body.

With a pencil, draw a head shape. Add an oval for the body shape and sausages for the arms and legs. The body is about one and a half times as long as the head.

Add the outlines of the clothes, smoothing off any joins, such as between the arms or legs and the body. Go over the outline in ink and rub out pencil lines.

Add hands and feet and colour the figure in.

You can find out how to make your cartoon figure look as if it is moving on pages 12-15.

More cartoon people to draw

Try varying your rounded shapes or stick figures to draw different-shaped cartoon people.

Tiny person. Head larger in proportion to body.

Tall person. Egg-shaped head and longer body.

Fat person. Head squashed and legs shorter.

Short person. Head, body and legs the same length.

Some things to try

When you have practised drawing several figures using the methods shown above, you could try drawing a figure outline straight off. If you find it difficult, you can go back to drawing a stick or rounded shape figure first.

Try drawing these different people:
- A fat lady in a fur coat and hat.
- A man with hairy legs in shorts.
- A boy and a girl wearing party clothes.

Making faces

You can make cartoon characters come to life by giving them different expressions. These two pages show you how to do this, by adding or changing a few lines. First, try the faces in pencil. Then you can colour them in.

Happy faces

Girls and women tend to have slightly smaller noses than boys and men.

These lines make the ears look more real.

Happiness is shown by a smiling mouth. Drawing the eyes as shown above gives a cheerful expression.

You can make the person burst out laughing by opening the mouth more and showing the teeth.

This is a bigger laugh. The head is thrown back. You can find out how to position the features on page 3.

Sad and angry faces

Sadness and anger are also mainly shown in the eyes and mouth.

Lines show shaking with fury.

Sad: the mouth and eyebrows droop.

Angry: use straight lines for the mouth and eyebrows.

Furious: the person frowns and goes red in the face.

Hopping mad: the mouth is wide open in a loud yell.

More expressions

Here are lots more expressions for you to copy and practise.

Winking. Mouth tilts up on side where eye is closed.

You can make the face look fatter by adding curves on the cheeks and chin.

Yawning. Nose squashes up to eyes which are closed. Mouth is wide open showing teeth.

Sly. Eyes look sideways and mouth is pursed.

Thoughtful. Eyes look up and sideways.

Sickly. Face has a greenish tinge. Tongue hangs out. Eyes are creased up.

White stripes in hair make it look shiny.

Smug. Sideways grin and half-closed eyes.

Frightened. Face is pale and bluish. Hair stands on end. Eyes are wide open.

Frowning forehead and drooping mouth look worried.

A wavy line for the mouth and droopy eyes give a bored look.

This view of someone is called a three-quarter profile.

A white patch on the balloon makes it shiny.

Try drawing some of these expressions from different angles. See page 3 if you need help with positioning the features on the face.

Blowing up a balloon. Cheeks are full and eyes closed.

These lines make it look as if the balloon is getting bigger.

7

Drawing caricatures

A caricature is a picture of someone which exaggerates their most striking or unusual features. Although a caricature looks funny, you can recognize the person easily.

It helps to look at the person, or at a photograph of them, while you are drawing.

Caricatured features

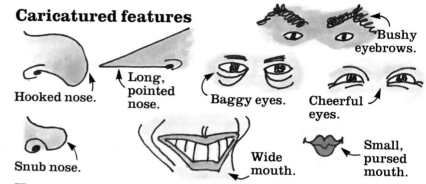

Hooked nose.

Long, pointed nose.

Snub nose.

Bushy eyebrows.

Baggy eyes.

Cheerful eyes.

Wide mouth.

Small, pursed mouth.

Here are some examples of caricatured features. You can copy or adapt them for your own caricatures.

Tricks of the trade

Imagine the features you would pick out if you were describing the person to someone else. These are the features to exaggerate.

Here are some caricatures drawn from photographs. Try copying them.

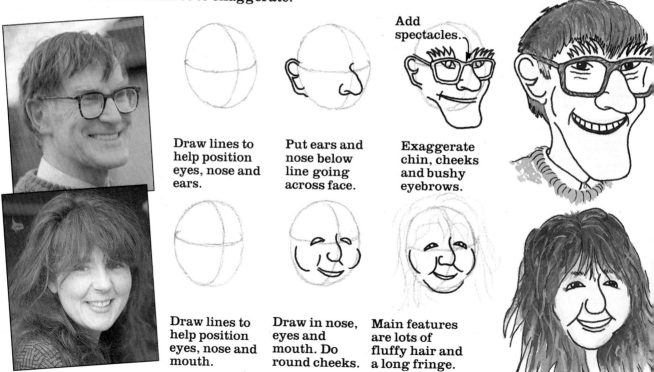

Add spectacles.

Draw lines to help position eyes, nose and ears.

Put ears and nose below line going across face.

Exaggerate chin, cheeks and bushy eyebrows.

Draw lines to help position eyes, nose and mouth.

Draw in nose, eyes and mouth. Do round cheeks.

Main features are lots of fluffy hair and a long fringe.

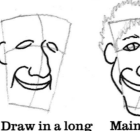

Draw a face shape and lines. Add ear and earring.

Do small, turned-up nose, glasses, and mouth.

Main features are cheeks, spiky hair and glasses.

Head is long and wedge-shaped rather than round.

Draw in a long nose, a smile, an ear and eyes.

Main features are cheeks, long chin and fluffy hair.

Round head. Lines show where eyes and nose go.

Draw a big nose, a grin, eyes and chubby cheeks.

Make chin a bit longer. Do a long fringe over eyes.

Caricature yourself

You can draw a funny caricature of yourself by looking at yourself in a shiny spoon. The curve of the spoon distorts your features.

If you look in the back of the spoon, your nose looks very big.

Turn the spoon sideways to get a different effect.

Drawing from different sides

Here you can find out how to draw people from the side and from the back as well as from the front.

You can also see how to make your pictures look interesting by drawing, say, a bird's eye view. There are some instructions for how to do this on the opposite page.

Turning round

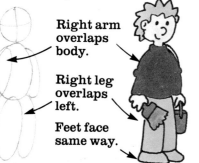

Right arm overlaps body.

Right leg overlaps left.

Feet face same way.

As a person begins to turn round, their body gets narrower. (See page 3 for how to draw the face.)

Side view

Arm towards back of body.

Shape of nose

Back of hand.

Left leg just visible behind right.

From the side, the body is at its narrowest. You can see the shape of the nose and the back of one hand.

Back view

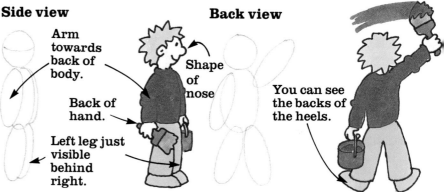

You can see the backs of the heels.

From the back, the body parts are the same sizes and shapes as from the front.

More positions to draw

Here are lots of cartoon people, in all sorts of positions. Copy them and they will help you draw people in other positions, too.

Sitting on the ground.

Piggy-back

On a bicycle.

Sitting on a chair.

Drawing a bird's eye view

A bird's eye view can make an ordinary picture look quite dramatic. Try drawing this queue.

The parts of the body nearer to you are bigger than those further away. Also, the bodies are shorter than if you were drawing them from straight on. This is called foreshortening.

Draw a set of pencil rules fanning out from a point. Fit the people roughly in between them.

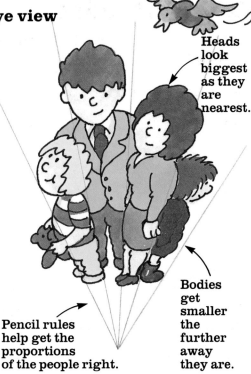

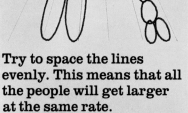

Heads look biggest as they are nearest.

Pencil rules help get the proportions of the people right.

Bodies get smaller the further away they are.

A worm's eye view

Bodies get smaller the further away they are and they are foreshortened.

A worm's eye view is from ground level. Draw another set of pencil rules starting from the top. This time, the people's feet are biggest.

The head of the tallest person is the smallest.

Looking from the bottom, the feet are biggest.

Hints for the pictures

Try to space the lines evenly. This means that all the people will get larger at the same rate.

Big people can slightly overlap the lines, and small people can fall within them.

The longer you draw the people, the more of a worm's eye view the picture will become. This is also true for a bird's eye view.

11

Moving pictures

Here, you can find out how to draw cartoon people walking, running, jumping and so on. Start with a stick or shape figure if it helps.

Walking and running

The right arm is in front when the left leg is forward.

Stick figure to help you get the body right.

Draw the figure just above ground level to show he is on the move.

Add a few curved lines to show fast movement.

Blobs of sweat flying off head.

When someone is walking briskly, they lean forwards slightly. There is always one foot on the ground.

Starting to run, the body leans forwards even more. The elbows bend and move backwards and forwards.

The faster someone is going, the more the body leans forwards and the further the arms stretch.

Jumping

The more this leg bends, the higher the jump will be.

Both feet come forward to hit the ground.

Running towards the jump . . .   Taking off . . .   In mid-flight . . .   Landing from the jump.

Falling over

These pictures show a stick person running along and tripping over. Copy them and then fill in the body shapes around the stick figures.

12

Action pictures

Here are lots of action pictures to try. There are stick figures next to each picture, to help you get the body right. Look at page 4 if you need reminding how long each part of the body should be.

Hitting

These curved lines show the swing of the racket.

Throwing

These lines show the path of the ball.

Diving

Lines show direction of movement.

Swimming

Add lots of splashes and movement lines.

Rollerskating

Arm stretched out in front.

Rollerskating is similar to running but there is always a foot on the ground.

Skateboarding

Body leaning back and legs bent.

You can get a good sense of turning a corner fast by bending the body and legs.

Kicking

When kicking a ball, the body twists towards the foot that is kicking.

13

More movement

Here are some even more dramatic ways to show movement. You exaggerate certain things to give an impression of lots of speed or effort. You can write words on a picture to give extra impact.

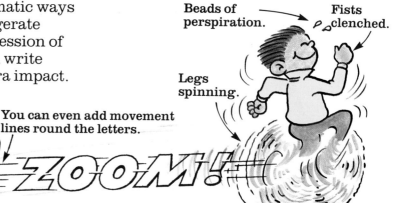

Beads of perspiration.

Fists clenched.

Legs spinning.

Clouds of dust.

You can even add movement lines round the letters.

ZOOM!

Make the letters big and bold. You could do them in colour.

This is someone running to catch a bus. You can add a word like ZOOM or WHIZZ, with an exclamation mark.

ZIP!

Wheel spin.

The hair and scarf of the skater on the left are streaming out behind her. This gives a sense of speed.

These figures look like they are running away. The dust clouds get smaller as they get further away.* The figures are in the distance, so they are small. A curved line for the ground gives a feeling of space.

These silhouettes have long shadows to make it look like evening.

14   *This is called perspective. There is more about it on pages 20-21, 59 and 117.*

Freeze-frame pictures

You can draw pictures that look frozen in the middle of exciting action, as if you were freezing a video during a film. You do this by adding details of moving things, such as those in the pictures here.

Wide mouth and eyes and spinning head make him look dazed.

Ski pole flying through the air makes it look like the accident has just happened.

Snow swooshing up as skier comes to a sudden halt.

An action scene to try

These lines make it look like the person is somersaulting.

Boy's purse falling from his pocket.

You could copy this picture, but try drawing different costumes, hairstyles and expressions.

Girl's drink spilling.

Try drawing someone trampolining. They might get into all sorts of positions in the air.

Some freeze-frame ideas

Scenes where there is a lot of action are good for freeze-frame pictures.

You could try an ice-rink, a windy day, or a party by a swimming pool.

15

Drawing stereotypes

As well as drawing caricatures of real people (see pages 8-9), you can draw caricatures of different types of people, such as a burglar or a chef. These are called stereotypes. They are not pictures of real people but you can recognize from the pictures what sort of people they are or what they do for a living.

You normally recognize a stereotype from the shape of the body and the clothes. Here are some to try.

(see pages 8-9)

Getting started

If you like, draw stick figures or rounded shapes to help you get started on the figure. There is more about this on pages 4-5. Then you can work on the outline and clothes.

Can you see which pictures on these two pages the shapes above belong to?

on pages 4-5.

Chef

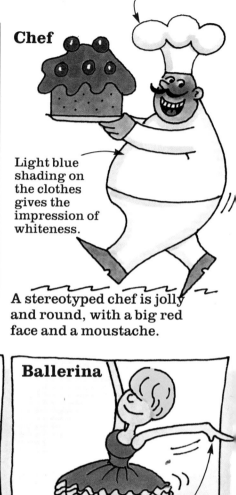

Chef's hat

Light blue shading on the clothes gives the impression of whiteness.

A stereotyped chef is jolly and round, with a big red face and a moustache.

Burglar

Swag bag

SWAG

Striped jersey

Torch

The burglar creeps along on tip-toe.

No real burglar would wear this kind of outfit, but this is how they are often drawn in cartoons.

Boxer

Head protected by hands.

Opponent knocked out.

The boxer is muscular and heavy, with a squashy nose and swollen ear. He wears big gloves and laced boots.

Ballerina

These lines show she is pirouetting.

Slender limbs and hands.

The ballerina is very slim and light on her feet. She stands on her toes.

Spy

The spy's hat is pulled down and the collar of his coat is turned up. One furtive eye looks out from under the brim of his hat.

Pop star

A pop star wears trendy clothes and jewellery. Draw her mouth open and coloured lights behind her.

Soccer player

A soccer player looks fit and energetic. You can draw him wearing your favourite team's strip.

Jockey

Jodphurs

Riding crop

A jockey is small, wiry and bow-legged. He wears a peaked hat with the brim turned up and racing colours on his clothes.

Gangster

Dark glasses

A gangster wears smart clothes, smokes a cigar and carries a violin case to conceal his gun.

More stereotypes

Clown

Fairytale princess

Cowboy

Witch

Butler

Here are some ideas for some more stereotypes. Can you think of others?

17

Cartoons growing up

As people grow older, their bodies change shape. So does the way they stand, sit and move.

These pages show some of the tricks involved in drawing people of different ages.

Babies

Wisp of hair.

High, round forehead.

Eyes half way down face.

Ears level with nose.

Toothy grin.

Legs and arms are short and chubby.

You can exaggerate the size of the mouth.

Babies sit with their legs straight out.

The face shape is a circle. The features are all in the lower half of the face.

A baby's shape is rounded with a large head, a bulge for a nappy and short limbs.

A baby's head is about one third of the whole length of the body.

Children

Eyebrows placed well above the eyes make the eyes look open and lively.

A lopsided grin looks cheeky.

Children's bodies are still quite rounded.

Children's heads are still quite large in proportion to the rest of the body.

Ears and nose half way down head.

Eyes slightly above line of ears.

There is slightly more space between the chin and mouth on a child than on a baby.

Girls' and boys' faces are similar shapes but they can have different hairstyles.

As a child grows, the limbs get longer in proportion to the rest of the body.

Men and women

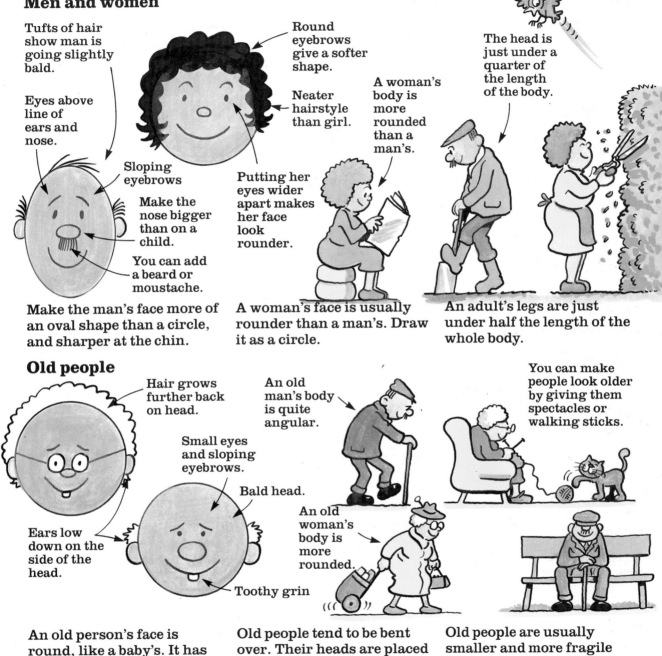

Tufts of hair show man is going slightly bald.

Eyes above line of ears and nose.

Sloping eyebrows

Round eyebrows give a softer shape.

Neater hairstyle than girl.

Make the nose bigger than on a child.

You can add a beard or moustache.

Make the man's face more of an oval shape than a circle, and sharper at the chin.

A woman's body is more rounded than a man's.

Putting her eyes wider apart makes her face look rounder.

A woman's face is usually rounder than a man's. Draw it as a circle.

The head is just under a quarter of the length of the body.

An adult's legs are just under half the length of the whole body.

Old people

Hair grows further back on head.

Ears low down on the side of the head.

Small eyes and sloping eyebrows.

Bald head.

Toothy grin

An old man's body is quite angular.

An old woman's body is more rounded.

You can make people look older by giving them spectacles or walking sticks.

An old person's face is round, like a baby's. It has other similar features.

Old people tend to be bent over. Their heads are placed further forwards.

Old people are usually smaller and more fragile than younger adults.

19

Scenery and perspective

Scenery and backgrounds can add a lot of information about what is happening in your pictures. You need to keep the scenery quite simple, though, so that characters stand out against it.

Here, you can see how to get a sense of distance, or depth, into pictures. This is called drawing in perspective.*

Tricks of perspective

The further away something is, the smaller it looks. The woman in this picture is drawn smaller than the burglar to make her look further away.

Draw the woman further up the picture than the burglar. Otherwise it will look like the picture above. She just looks like a tiny person.

Parallel lines appear to get closer the further away they are. They seem to meet on the horizon. This point is called the vanishing point.

A high vanishing point makes it seem as if you are looking down on the picture. What happens if you draw a low vanishing point?

A picture in perspective

Here is a picture in perspective. The woman is drawn smaller and further up than the burglar to make her look further away.

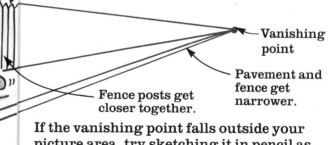

Vanishing point

Pavement and fence get narrower.

Fence posts get closer together.

If the vanishing point falls outside your picture area, try sketching it in pencil as above. This helps to get all the lines properly in perspective. You can rub the lines out later.

There is more about perspective on page 59.

Adding depth

Lines going across a picture can also add depth. Here, the lines of hills make it look as if the scenery goes back for miles.

See how the road gets narrower in perspective as it gets further away, and the birds get smaller.

Scenery gets paler and less distinct the further away it is.

The man is large because he is nearest to you.

◄ In this picture, the curved lines of the circus arena show the depth of the picture.

Colour and shape are less distinct the further away they are, so only the front row of people are drawn in. Coloured blobs suggest the rest of the crowd.

Drawing objects

Wheels support engine.

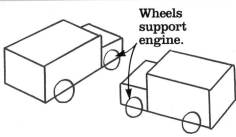

Rub out these lines.

Square or oblong objects, such as tables and chairs, are quite easy to draw in perspective. The opposite sides are almost parallel.

You can draw a more complicated object, such as a car, by first constructing it out of a number of box shapes.

Then round off the corners and add the details. You may need to practise this a bit. Looking at an object while you draw it can help.

Cartoon jokes

Cartoon jokes are often printed in black and white in newspapers and magazines. They may be in the form of a strip (see pages 24-25) or a single picture, called a single cartoon. The one on the right is a single cartoon.

Here you can find out what kind of jokes make good cartoons, what materials cartoonists use and some tips on drawing single cartoons yourself.

What makes a good single cartoon?

Visual, that is, a lot of the humour and information about what is happening is in the picture.

A short caption.

A joke that is quick and easy to get.

The type of joke that makes a good single cartoon usually has the qualities shown above.

Ideas for jokes

It can be difficult to think up ideas for jokes on the spot. It helps to think first of a theme or situation. This may then suggest something funny to you.

Here are some common cartoon themes and some jokes based on them.

A desert island

This is probably the most common theme for single cartoon jokes.

A hospital

This joke has two common cartoon themes – hospitals and manhole covers.

Vampires

This is funny because it shows a monstrous creature doing something ordinary.

Drawing materials*

The materials shown below are enough to get you started. You may already have them. If you like, though, you can buy the more specialized materials shown on the rest of this page.

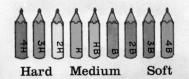

Hard   Medium   Soft

Pencils are marked to show how hard or soft they are. Experiment to find a type you like. Pencils range from 9B (very soft) to 9H (very hard).

You can draw on good quality typing paper which is quite cheap.

Fibre tip pens do not smudge or blot. In time, though, the ink fades in daylight. If you find it easier, sketch a drawing in pencil first and then ink over it. You can cover mistakes with typewriter correction fluid.

How professional cartoonists work

Single cartoons are drawn in black and white for printing in newspapers and magazines. Here are some of the materials that cartoonists use. You could try some of them yourself.

Pencils. The artist might use a medium pencil for outlines and a softer one for shading.

Fine paintbrushes

Art board. This can have different surfaces from very smooth and shiny to quite rough and soft.

Fibre tip pens

Cartoons are mostly printed quite small. They are usually drawn larger than final size and reduced photographically before printing.

The cartoonist is told what size the cartoon will be printed.
By drawing a diagonal line across a box that size, the artist can scale the size up so that it is larger but still the same shape.

Drawing pens. These come with different thicknesses of nib. They draw a very even line.

Dip pens and Indian ink. You can get different shapes and thicknesses of nib.

Cartridge paper takes pens, pencils or paint equally well.

Fountain pens

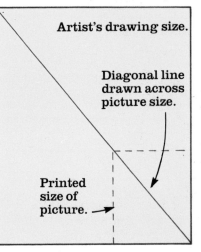

Artist's drawing size.

Diagonal line drawn across picture size.

Printed size of picture.

Strip cartoons

A strip cartoon is a joke told in more than one frame. Like a single cartoon, the joke needs to be visual. It can be like a short story with a punchline.

One of the hardest things about drawing a strip cartoon is making characters look the same in each frame. To start with, only use one or two characters. Give them features which you find easy to draw.

How to start

Close-ups varied with larger scenes.

As with single cartoons, think of a theme first and make up a joke around it.

Divide the joke up into three or four stages. You can vary the sizes of the frames, and close-ups with larger scenes, to make the strip look more interesting.

Speech bubbles

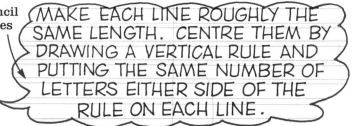

Put bubbles over background areas with no detail.

You can put speech and thoughts in bubbles in the pictures. These can be different shapes. The shape of the bubble may suggest the way something is being said.

Keep the speech short or the strip gets complicated and the bubbles take up too much room. Make sure you allow room for bubbles when you sketch out the pictures.

Pencil rules

It is best to do the lettering before you draw the bubble outline. Use a pen with a fine tip.

To get the letters the same height, draw parallel pencil rules and letter in between them, as above. Then rub out the pencil lines. The letters are likely to be quite small, so it is best to use capital letters which are easier to read.

A finished strip

This strip is about a caveman. He is quite an easy character to repeat from frame to frame because of his simple features and clothing.*

Speech bubble over the sky area.

Different sized frames make strip more interesting.

Sound effects make the strip more fun. As you read it you imagine the noises so it is a bit like watching a film.

Bright colours make the characters stand out. The background is paler.

A lot of the humour in a strip cartoon comes from the expressions on the characters faces.

When positioning speech bubbles, remember that people read from left to right down the frame. They will read bubbles at the top before they read bubbles further down.

Borders for the strip

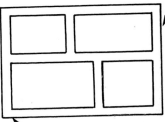

Border round strip.

Use a ruler and a pen with a slightly thicker tip than the one you used for the lettering. You can put the whole strip in a larger box.

Freehand borders are finished off without a ruler.

1. Place a ruler just below where you want to draw the line.

2. Run your fingers along the ruler as you paint. (You may need to practise this.)

The borders round the frames can make a strip look neat and tidy or free and artistic. Here are some ideas for different borders.

Freehand borders give a sketchy effect. To keep them straight, draw the lines in pencil with a ruler. Then go over them in ink.

Paintbrush borders are nice because the line varies slightly in thickness. You can get a straight line using the method above.

*You can find out how to draw dinosaurs on pages 46-47.

Comic strips

You may have your own favourite comics. The stories in them are fun to read because there is very little text and a lot of action in the pictures.

These two pages describe how a comic strip artist creates a comic strip. You could try making up your own comic strip in the same way.

Creating a comic strip

A practical joke . . . an escape from the zoo . . . an arctic expedition . . . a kidnap!

The first thing to do when creating a comic strip is to think of a plot. It needs to be funny or dramatic – or both. The plot needs an exciting finish.

Bad-tempered.

Tough and reliable.

Lively and clever.

Grumbling and lazy.

The characters need strong personalities which will come across in the pictures. You can tell what the characters above are like just from looking at them.

Find out how to use special effects to add excitement to your pictures on pages 28-29.

The plot needs to be full of action to keep the reader interested. The story needs to move fast and something new must happen in each picture.

Writing a script

A script explains what is happening in each frame of the comic strip. It describes the scenery, what the characters are doing and saying and any sound effects. Some artists write their own scripts. Others illustrate scripts written by someone else.

The page of a comic is a fixed size so the story needs to be divided up into the right number of frames to fit on it.

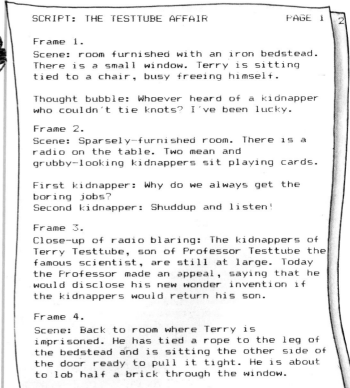

```
SCRIPT: THE TESTTUBE AFFAIR                    PAGE 1

Frame 1.
Scene: room furnished with an iron bedstead.
There is a small window. Terry is sitting
tied to a chair, busy freeing himself.

Thought bubble: Whoever heard of a kidnapper
who couldn't tie knots? I've been lucky.

Frame 2.
Scene: Sparsely-furnished room. There is a
radio on the table. Two mean and
grubby-looking kidnappers sit playing cards.

First kidnapper: Why do we always get the
boring jobs?
Second kidnapper: Shuddup and listen!

Frame 3.
Close-up of radio blaring: The kidnappers of
Terry Testtube, son of Professor Testtube the
famous scientist, are still at large. Today
the Professor made an appeal, saying that he
would disclose his new wonder invention if
the kidnappers would return his son.

Frame 4.
Scene: Back to room where Terry is
imprisoned. He has tied a rope to the leg of
the bedstead and is sitting the other side of
the door ready to pull it tight. He is about
to lob half a brick through the window.

Terry: This ought to fool those two idiots.
```

Drawing the strip

Here you can see how the script on the left (you can only see the first page) was made into a finished comic strip. It was drawn using a dip pen with a sprung nib. The nib gives a varying thickness of line depending on how hard it is pressed.

The story is mainly told in the pictures but there are bubbles for speech and thoughts.

Pressure on nib gives a thick line.

Frame sizes are varied to make strip more interesting.

A line of text at the top can explain changes of scene or time lapses.

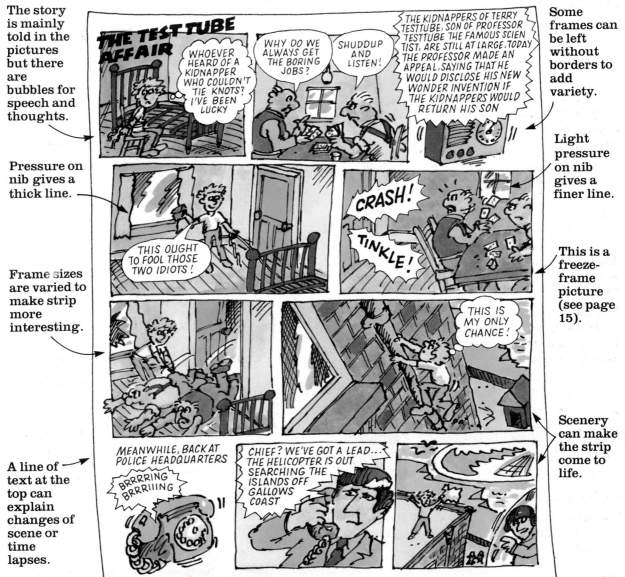

Some frames can be left without borders to add variety.

Light pressure on nib gives a finer line.

This is a freeze-frame picture (see page 15).

Scenery can make the strip come to life.

27

Special effects

Special effects can make cartoons look exciting. Here are some ideas for how to add drama and atmosphere to your pictures. You can make them spooky, mysterious, shocking or scary. You can also find out how to add sound effects.

Sound effects

You can add sound effects by using words and shapes which suggest the sound. The most common ones are explosions but there are lots of others you can use.

Jagged speech bubble suggests shock.

Shadows and silhouettes

Using different lighting effects for night pictures can make them look creepy or mysterious. Here are some suggestions:

Silhouettes in a lighted window. These are made by people sitting in front of a source of light.

Huge shadow on wall.

Silhouette of a castle in a thunderstorm.

28

Scary effects

This picture uses the effect of a harmless tree that looks scary in the dark. You could try a similar picture using a hat and coat hanging up to look like a sinister person.

Lines suggesting speed.

This type of shading, where you use lots of lines close together, is called hatching.*

Two strip cartoons

These strip cartoons use some of the special effects described on these pages.

1

MIIIAAAOOOW!

BOOM!

BANK MANAGER'S LUNCH BOX

2

CLOMP! CLOMP!

CLOMP! CLOMP!

A strip cartoon to try

Here is a script for a strip cartoon involving special effects for you to try.
Frame 1: Silhouettes of people by a bonfire.
Frame 2: Boy dressed up as a ghost frightens them away.

Frame 3: Boy takes sheet off and is shocked to hear laughter coming from a spooky tree silhouette.
Sound effect: HO HO HO

*You can find out about other ways to shade on page 71.

Cartoon story books

Cartoon stories are like long comic strips. The story is told in pictures with lots of action and excitement.

Tintin is one of the best known cartoon story characters. He and his dog, Snowy, first appeared in 1929 as a comic strip serial in a weekly children's newspaper. Later, the stories were made into magazines and books.

Who created Tintin?

Tintin

Snowy

Professor Calculus

Captain Haddock

Characters in the Tintin stories.*

One of the identical twin detectives, Thomson and Thompson.

A Belgian man called Hergé created Tintin. Hergé's real name was Georges Remi. The name Hergé came from the French pronunciation of his initials, G.R., backwards. He was born in 1907 and died in 1983.

The Studios Hergé

Until the early 1940s, Hergé worked alone on Tintin. Later he assembled a team to help colour in the pictures, letter the speech bubbles and so on. This team became known as the Studios Hergé. All the stories were thoroughly researched so that details of costume, architecture, machinery and so on were correct.

The ship Unicorn, from *The Secret of the Unicorn* and *Red Rackham's Treasure* was based on ships in the French navy in the 17th century.*

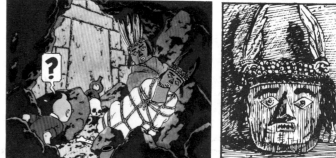

The Inca masks in this picture from *Prisoners of the Sun*, were based on the sketch on the right.*

Sketch by a 19th century explorer of Peru and Bolivia.

First Hergé wrote a plot and sketched the drawings. He then worked on the drawings, redrawing them as many as ten times. The drawings were then handed to his assistants. They filled in backgrounds, coloured the pictures and drew and lettered the speech bubbles. Hergé drew all the characters and checked the final pictures.

Hergé's techniques

The Tintin books have a very distinctive style. Here you can see some of its features in a section from *Prisoners of the Sun*.

Many of them add variety to the picture strips so that they look lively, exciting and never boring.*

Unusual angles look dramatic and make the story more interesting.
▼

The pictures are clear and the outlines are unbroken.
▼

Hergé varied the sizes of frames to add variety and suit the picture.
▼

The faces show many different expressions.
▼

Colours are clear and flat with no shading.
▼

▲ Costumes and scenery were thoroughly researched so that all details were correct.

▲ Background colours are plain and muted. The bright costumes stand out against them.

▲ Hergé varied close-ups with larger pictures of single characters and scenes with lots of people.

The stories are full of suspense and drama. This is because they were first published in newspaper serials. Hergé needed to create suspense at the end of each instalment.

Drawing animals

You can draw animals in a similar way to drawing people, by using simple shapes and lines and adding features.

Animals make good cartoons because you can use their natural characteristics, such as claws, tails, ears and so on to give them personality. Here are lots of animals to draw.*

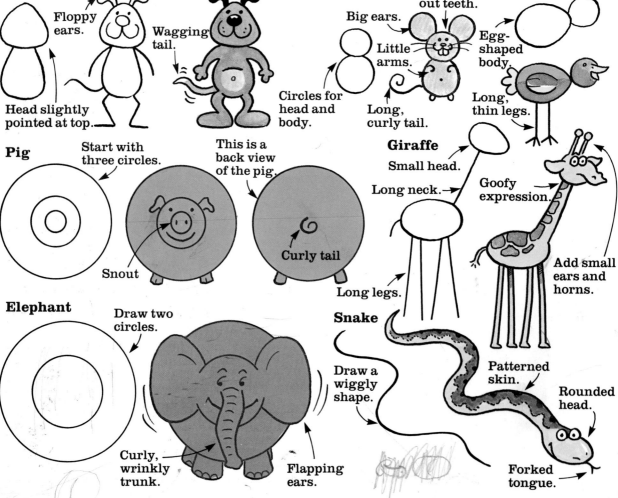

Cat

Round head.

Egg-shaped body.

Add face, ears and sticks for arms and legs.

Dog

Floppy ears.

Wagging tail.

Head slightly pointed at top.

Pig

Start with three circles.

This is a back view of the pig.

Snout

Curly tail

Elephant

Draw two circles.

Curly, wrinkly trunk.

Flapping ears.

Mouse

Big ears.

Sticking out teeth.

Little arms.

Circles for head and body.

Long, curly tail.

Bird

Egg-shaped body.

Long, thin legs.

Giraffe

Small head.

Long neck.

Goofy expression.

Long legs.

Add small ears and horns.

Snake

Draw a wiggly shape.

Patterned skin.

Rounded head.

Forked tongue.

*You can find out how to turn animals into monsters on pages 64-65.

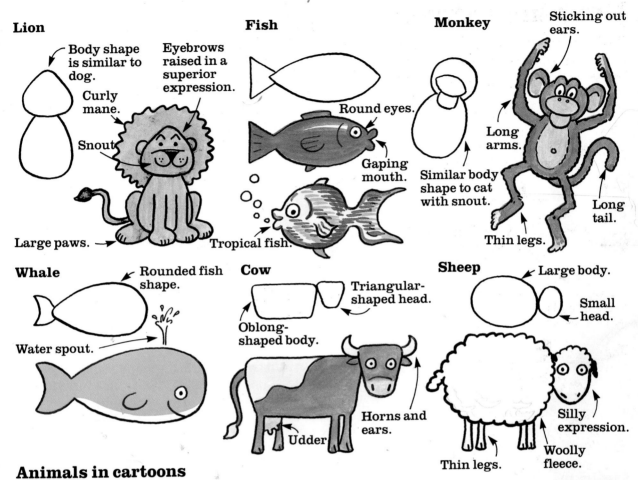

Lion

Body shape is similar to dog.

Curly mane.

Snout

Large paws.

Eyebrows raised in a superior expression.

Fish

Round eyes.

Gaping mouth.

Tropical fish.

Monkey

Sticking out ears.

Long arms.

Similar body shape to cat with snout.

Thin legs.

Long tail.

Whale

Rounded fish shape.

Water spout.

Cow

Triangular-shaped head.

Oblong-shaped body.

Horns and ears.

Udder

Sheep

Large body.

Small head.

Silly expression.

Woolly fleece.

Thin legs.

Animals in cartoons

Cartoons may look very violent but usually no real harm is done. The cartoon below might help you think up a few of your own animal cartoons.

SPLAT!

How cartoon films are made

The most famous cartoon film maker in the world was Walt Disney. He made such films as Mickey Mouse and Bambi. He started work in the 1920s. Although equipment and materials have improved over the years, the way cartoon films are made has changed very little.

On the next four pages you can find out how cartoon films are made. This is called cartoon animation.

How film works

Projector shines light through film.

You see the film projected on to a film screen.

Projector magnifies film.

Shutter comes down in between each frame.

There are 24 frames for each second of film — that makes 864,000 frames per hour.

Film is wound on.

A film is a sequence of tiny pictures, or frames. There are 24 frames for each second of film. A projector shines light through them and magnifies them.

Each frame is held still in front of the projector just long enough for you to see it. Then a shutter comes down while the next frame is positioned.

This happens so fast that you do not notice individual frames or the shutter. Without the shutter between frames, the film would look like a long blur.

Making the film

A cartoon film is made by taking photos of thousands of drawings. The drawings show all the different stages of movement.

The photos of the drawings are combined into a film strip. (There is more about how all this is done over the page.)

Each photo makes one frame. 24 frames make one second of the film. Below, you can see the frames in one second of a film.

24 frames make one second of film.

Planning the film

The story of the film is divided up into scenes. The artists working on the film, called the animators, do a set of drawings. This shows what happens in each scene. It is called a storyboard.

The storyboard is a bit like a strip cartoon. What the characters are saying is written under the pictures.

Storyboard

Animating the film

The animators break each scene down into different movements. Then, each animator works on drawing one movement at a time: for instance, a sneeze.

The animator draws the start and end of the sneeze and a few of the main stages in between.

These pictures are called key pictures. Each key picture is numbered. The numbers show how many other stages need to be drawn in between to complete the sneeze.

Key pictures

The animator has a chart showing what will happen during each split second of the film — action, speech, sound effects and music. The movements drawn are matched to the sound.

Chart

Look over the page to see what happens next.

35

Completing the drawings

Key picture

In-betweener adds these pictures.

Key picture

Once all the key pictures have been drawn, they are passed on to other members of the animating team.

These members are called in-betweeners because they do the drawings in between the key pictures.

The numbers on the key pictures show the in-betweener how many more pictures are needed.

How the artists work

Each animator or in-betweener works on a flat box with a glass surface, called a light box.

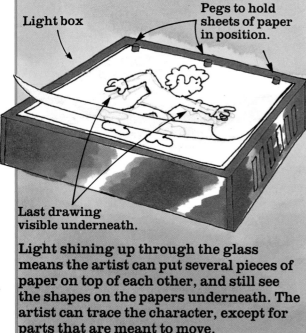

Light box

Pegs to hold sheets of paper in position.

Last drawing visible underneath.

Light shining up through the glass means the artist can put several pieces of paper on top of each other, and still see the shapes on the papers underneath. The artist can trace the character, except for parts that are meant to move.

Tracing and colouring

The finished drawings are traced on to transparent sheets called cels.

Each cel is then turned over and painted on the back, so that brush strokes do not show on the front. The cels are now ready for the next stage, when they are photographed. This stage is called shooting.

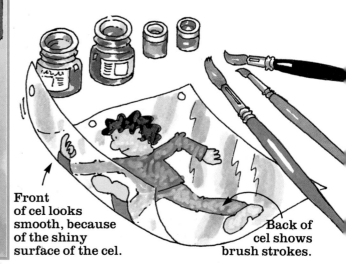

Front of cel looks smooth, because of the shiny surface of the cel.

Back of cel shows brush strokes.

Background scenery

Background scenery is painted on long rolls of paper. During shooting, the scenery is laid on the plate of a rostrum camera (see right). The cel with the character drawn on it is placed on top of it.

Background scenery

Cel with character drawn on it.

Each time a new cel is put on the plate, the background scenery can be moved to either side. This makes it look as if the character is moving.

Background scenery rolls this way.

The character stays in the same place on the plate of the camera, but the scenery is moved behind him. This makes it look as if he is running along.

Rostrum camera

The type of camera used to take photographs for a cartoon film is called a rostrum camera. One cel at a time is placed on the plate of the camera and a picture taken. All the photos are combined into one reel of film.

Rostrum camera plate.

Flick the pages and watch your cartoon say hello.

Animate your own cartoon

Use a small notebook with thin paper so you can see the line of a black felt tip pen through the page.

Hold the notebook firmly closed. Draw three thick, black lines across the tops of all the pages.

On the first page, copy the picture above. Tear it out. Number the next ten pages from one to ten.

Trace your picture on to pages one and ten. Use the marks at the top of the page to line the pages up.

On page five, trace the head, but make him raise his hat. You now have three key pictures.

Draw the in-between stages. Start with page nine and work back. Trace parts staying still.

Mix and match

Here are lots of pictures of heads, bodies and legs from different sides. You can copy them and use them in your own pictures. Remember that a person's head might be facing you while the body is sideways on, and vice versa.

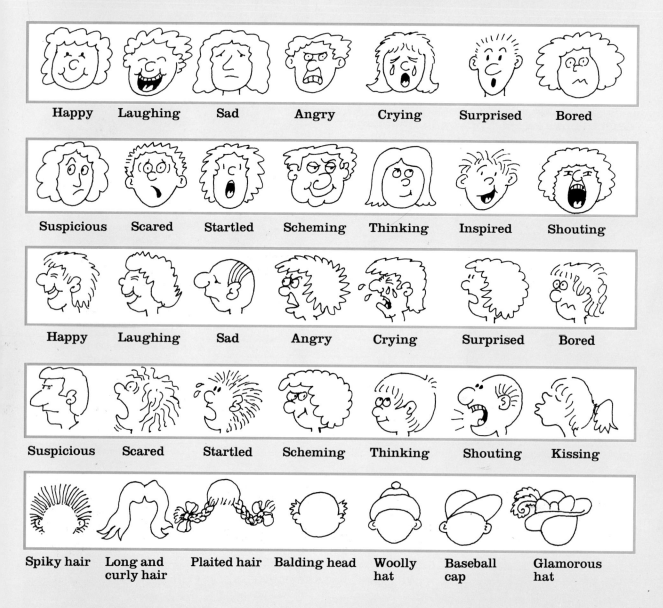

Happy   Laughing   Sad   Angry   Crying   Surprised   Bored

Suspicious   Scared   Startled   Scheming   Thinking   Inspired   Shouting

Happy   Laughing   Sad   Angry   Crying   Surprised   Bored

Suspicious   Scared   Startled   Scheming   Thinking   Shouting   Kissing

Spiky hair   Long and curly hair   Plaited hair   Balding head   Woolly hat   Baseball cap   Glamorous hat

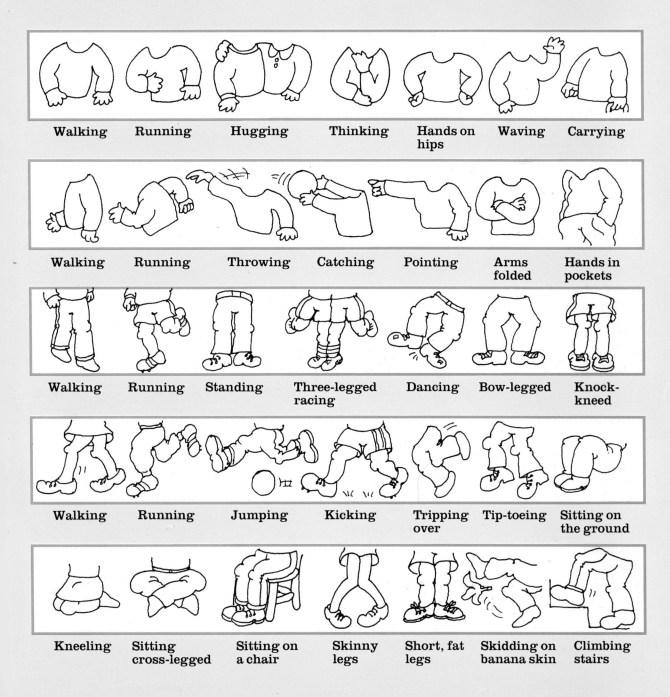

Walking Running Hugging Thinking Hands on hips Waving Carrying

Walking Running Throwing Catching Pointing Arms folded Hands in pockets

Walking Running Standing Three-legged racing Dancing Bow-legged Knock-kneed

Walking Running Jumping Kicking Tripping over Tip-toeing Sitting on the ground

Kneeling Sitting cross-legged Sitting on a chair Skinny legs Short, fat legs Skidding on banana skin Climbing stairs

Cartoons and real people

Cartoons look friendly and funny. They have big heads, hands and feet and you can easily give them funny expressions. They have a cuddly, rounded shape. The rules for drawing real people are different, as you can see on this page.

Heads

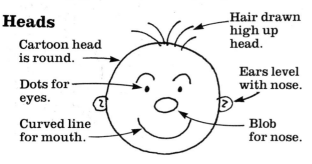

Cartoon head is round.

Dots for eyes.

Curved line for mouth.

Hair drawn high up head.

Ears level with nose.

Blob for nose.

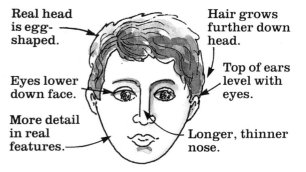

Real head is egg-shaped.

Eyes lower down face.

More detail in real features.

Hair grows further down head.

Top of ears level with eyes.

Longer, thinner nose.

A cartoon nose goes in the middle of the face. A real nose is long rather than blob-shaped and the nostrils are low down the face.

Real eyes are lower down the face than cartoon eyes. Cartoon ears are level with the nose. Real ears are more level with the eyes.

Cartoon features are simple and you do not need to shade cartoon heads. They usually look quite flat. You shade a real head to give it shape.

Bodies

The proportions of cartoon people are different to those of real people. A whole cartoon body is about four times as long as its head. A real body is seven or eight times as long as its head.

Hands and feet are usually bigger on a cartoon and the body shape is more rounded. Look at the differences on the right.

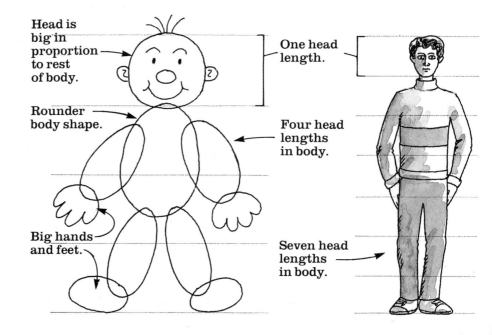

Head is big in proportion to rest of body.

Rounder body shape.

Big hands and feet.

One head length.

Four head lengths in body.

Seven head lengths in body.

40

Part 2
HOW TO DRAW
MONSTERS
AND OTHER CREATURES

Cheryl Evans

Designed and illustrated by Graham Round and Kim Blundell

Additional design and illustration by Brian Robertson and Jan Nesbitt

Contents

Consultant: Jocelyn Clarke

About part two

Monsters come in all shapes and sizes. They can be quite simple or fairly tricky to draw. This part of the book shows you how to draw lots of different monsters and colour them to make them look really dramatic.

Shapes to use.

Monster shapes
There are some ideas for monster shapes to start you drawing on pages 44-45.

Famous monsters

King Kong

Some of the most famous monsters in the world are here, too. Try drawing the Minotaur (page 63) or King Kong (page 65).

Dinosaur

All kinds of monsters
There are all kinds of monsters. For example, there are dinosaurs on pages 46-47, space aliens on pages 50-51, and giants on pages 58-59.

Fuzzy alien

Vac-dragon

Unusual monsters
You can turn anything into a monster. Try a vacuum cleaner (page 54), a blob (page 51) or a computer (page 69).

Scary settings
Scenery can make your monsters more exciting. See how to do a watery background for sea monsters on page 53, or a spooky graveyard on page 49, for instance.

Things to use
In this part of the book, you will see how to use pencils, felt-tips, crayons, chalk and other materials. There is a chart at the back to remind you of all the different things you can do.

Getting ideas

Some of the best monsters come from your own imagination. On this page there are pictures of the kinds of things that can inspire you. You will find ways to use ideas like these later in the book.

◀ Look for monsters in science fiction or horror films, television adventure programmes and cartoon films. Monsters can be funny or friendly as well as frightening.

Monsters have been around ▶ for thousands of years in myths and stories from all over the world. You can read about many strange beasts in books about mythology or collections of fairy tales.

This is Cerberus, the three-headed dog that guarded the entrance to the Underworld in Greek myths.

Gargoyle

You can make monsters ▶ from real animals by exaggerating certain things, such as teeth and claws, or their size. Even plants can be monstrous if you make them so.

This is a plant that eats insects, called a sundew. Can you imagine one so big it could eat people?

This cockroach looks armour-plated. You could do a monster's body like this.

Look out for monster ▶ ideas as you walk around outside. Cars, trees, cloud shapes or the ugly statues, called gargoyles, on some old buildings may inspire you, for example.

43

Monster shapes

Here are some ideas for monster shapes. Find out below how the shape of a monster can make it look frightening or friendly or make your skin crawl.

Straight lines and angles look unfriendly.

Try drawing a monster using only straight lines. It is more likely to look fierce than friendly. You could start from an animal shape. Draw it with straight lines, then add spikes on its back, pointed teeth and so on.

Four legs, head and tail, like an animal.

Dip your fingers in paint and make prints on the paper. Then you can turn your fingerprints into funny monsters. Add eyes, hair, horns, tails and so on with felt tips or crayons.

Round shapes look soft and friendly.

Shapes to make you shudder

One way to choose scary monster shapes is to think what makes people shudder. For instance, many people don't like spiders or snakes. You can find out how to draw this snake monster on the opposite page and in the labels around the picture.

Frowning eyebrows and mean, narrow eyes look angry.

Sharp horn

Long, thin, wiggly shapes can look slithery and unpleasant.

Use bright colours to make patterns.

Slit pupils, sharp fangs and a pointed tongue are like a fierce wild animal's.

A monster's face shows whether it is nice or nasty. This snake monster's face has pointed features and a fierce expression, like a dangerous wild animal's.

44

Draw a snake monster

Draw a wiggly line. Follow it with another line close to it. Add a pointed tail at one end and a fierce head at the other. Colour it in.

Pointed tail ➝

A friendly monster

Mop of hair looks soft.

Big, round eyes like a baby.

Blunt teeth are not as scary as sharp ones.

Upward-curving mouth makes a smile.

Rounded shapes are friendlier than sharp, spiky ones. This monster's cuddly body, big, round eyes and smiling mouth make it look cheerful and lovable.

Mixed monsters

If you mix shapes it can be hard to tell if the monster is nice or nasty. You could draw some mixed monster shapes of your own, like these ones, and try to decide if they are nice or not.

Round body, but sharp teeth and claws.

Sharp shapes for body, but smiling face.

45

Drawing dinosaurs

Dinosaurs were huge, real-life monsters that existed on Earth 150-200 million years ago. Here you can find out how to draw and colour some of them. You can adapt these basic shapes to make many others.*

Tyrannosaurus rex

Tyrannosaurus rex was the king of the meat-eating dinosaurs. It could grow to nearly 15 metres (49 feet) long. The picture in the box below shows you how to draw it. Hints for colouring and other details are shown on the right.

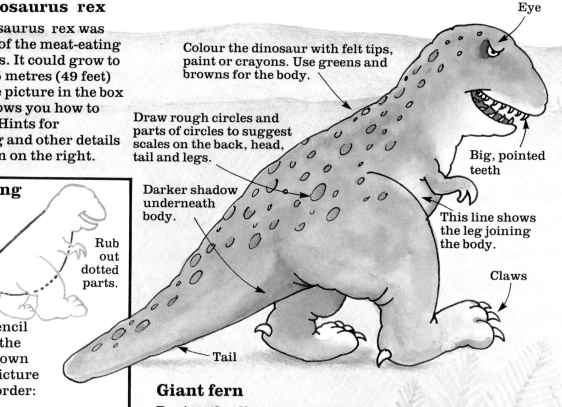

Colour the dinosaur with felt tips, paint or crayons. Use greens and browns for the body.

Draw rough circles and parts of circles to suggest scales on the back, head, tail and legs.

Darker shadow underneath body.

Eye

Big, pointed teeth

This line shows the leg joining the body.

Claws

Tail

Drawing the shape

Rub out dotted parts.

Use a pencil to copy the lines shown in the picture in this order:

—— First, the black lines.
—— Next, the orange lines.
—— Then the blue lines.

The boxes on page 47 show you how to draw two more dinosaurs. Copy the lines in the same order – black, then orange, then blue.

Giant fern

During the dinosaur period the Earth was warm and covered in dense forests. Plants were giant-sized, though many of them were like forest plants today.

Try drawing giant ferns, like this one, as a setting for your dinosaurs. Do curved lines for stems. Add narrow leaves on each side. The leaves get shorter towards the tip of each stem.

*There is a dinosaur in a strip cartoon on page 25.

Flying monsters

At the same time as the dinosaurs, there were also flying reptiles, like this pterodactyl. Copy the lines in the box below to draw it.

Sharp teeth

Scaly body like tyrannosaurus rex. Use brown paint or felt tip.

Use crayons for the wings (see below). This contrasts well with the body.

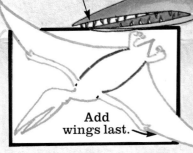

Add wings last.

Wing texture

The pterodactyl has bat-like wings. Get this effect by putting a leaf face-down under the paper and rubbing over it with a brown crayon.

Use a leaf with veins that stick out. A horse-chestnut or maple is good.

Diplodocus

This is a diplodocus. See ▶ how to draw it in the box below.

You can use the diplodocus shape, or any of the shapes on this page, as a base for drawing other monsters.

Use greys for the diplodocus.

Add an eye and a mouth.

Put a black shadow underneath the body.

Go over darker parts twice.

Diplodocus skin

To get a wrinkly skin texture as in this picture, put a sheet of rough sandpaper under your drawing and colour over the top with crayons. Press quite hard. Wax crayons look brighter than pencil crayons.

47

Spooky monsters

Ghosts are scary because nobody knows exactly what they are or if they even exist. Some people say they are shadowy, almost see-through shapes that appear in the dark. Here are some different kinds for you to try.

Floating ghost

Front view

Side view

This floating ghost shape looks a bit like someone with a sheet over their head and arms raised.

Give it a rounded head and wiggly "tail" where its feet would be so it looks as though it is fading away.

Draw the floor below the "tail" so the ghost seems to float.

You can only see one eye from the side.

Arms raised in a haunting gesture.

If you bend the "tail" to the back, it looks as though the ghost is going forwards.

Floor

Changing the shape

You can change the shape of a ghost to make it do different things. Give it an expression, too. Try some of the ideas below.

◄ Make a ghost do something normal, like sitting and reading. You can see the chair through the ghost.

◄ Give a furious ghost hands on its hips and an angry face. Do frowning eyebrows and a straight line for a mouth. Red is a good angry colour.

Ghostly colours

Here's one good way to do ghostly colours: draw the outline in felt tip. Then smudge the line with a wet paintbrush and spread the colour inside the shape.

Expressions to try

Why not try some ghostly expressions? Here are some tips to help you.*

Friendly: round eyes, curved eyebrows, and a smile. ▶

Surprised: open mouth, round eyes, raised eyebrows. ▶

Sad: eyebrows and eyes slope, mouth curves down. ▶

48 *There is more about expressions on pages 6-7.*

Graveyard phantom

Follow these stages to draw this spooky phantom in an eerie graveyard. It is easier to do than it may look.

1. Make a charcoal patch on white paper with a charcoal pencil or stick.

2. With a rubber, rub out a ghost shape, gravestones and blades of grass.

3. Add details with charcoal as in the picture.

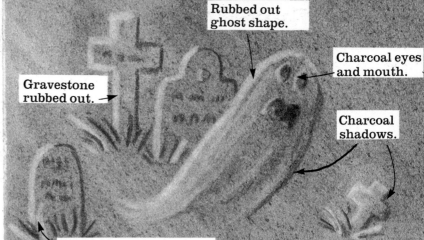

Rubbed out ghost shape.

Charcoal eyes and mouth.

Gravestone rubbed out.

Charcoal shadows.

Grass shapes rubbed out.

Headless spectre

Here is another type of ghost. It is in historical costume and has its head under its arm. To draw one like it, use white chalk on black paper. The instructions below should help.

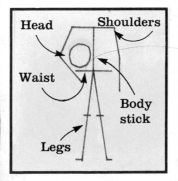

Head

Shoulders

Waist

Body stick

Legs

With a pencil, draw a stick man like this on your paper. Do legs twice as long as the body. Draw the head half as long as the body and to one side. Add lines for waist, shoulders and arms.

Join shoulders and waist. Do neck ruff, bloomers and feet. Add details from the picture on the left. Rub out extra lines. Go over the outline in chalk, then smudge it gently with a finger.*

Stop further smudging with fixative spray (see pages 70 and 133). **49**

Space aliens

What do you think aliens from outer space look like? Are they like slightly odd people or completely different?

There are some different kinds of aliens here for you to try and some space backgrounds for them, too.

Little green Martian

1

2

3

4

1. To draw the Martian, start with rough pencil circles for his head, body and feet.

2 and 3. With your pencil, add the lines shown in red in these two pictures.

4. Rub out unwanted lines. Do the final outline in black and colour him in.

Double space scene

Here's a way to get two dramatic space scenes in one go. You need wax crayons, coloured chalks, a pencil and two sheets of white paper. Just follow the steps below.

For these pictures you need three layers of colour. Use chalk for the first layer. Cover a sheet of paper with bright patches of chalk as shown here.

Colour over the chalk with a bright wax crayon – orange or yellow, say. Do the third layer with a dark wax crayon such as blue or green. It will look a bit like this.

Lay a second sheet of paper on top of the one you have coloured. Draw stars, planets, space ships or aliens in pencil on the top sheet. Press quite hard.

Moon blobs

Make blob aliens by drawing blob shapes like those above and adding features to them. You and your friends could draw blobs for each other to turn into aliens.

Do an outer space scene by drawing blob monsters on the moon. Paint the moon's mountains and craters white and grey and do a black sky with stars. A good way to spray stars is to dip an old toothbrush in white paint. Hold it bristles-down over the paper and run a finger along the bristles.

These blobs have been made into aliens in the scene below.

Craters have steep sides and a flat top with a hole in it.

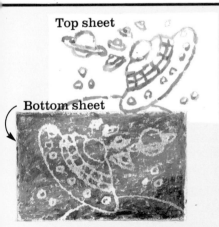

Top sheet

Bottom sheet

Remove the top sheet and turn it over. You now have two pictures. The one on the top sheet is made with wax crayon lifted from the other sheet by the pencil lines.

Friendly, fuzzy alien

This fuzzy alien looks soft and friendly. Use charcoal or a soft pencil to draw it. (Pencils can be hard or soft. Find out more about this on page 30.) This is what you do:

Draw a big nose.

Draw lines back and forwards like this. ➜

Move in a circle round the nose.

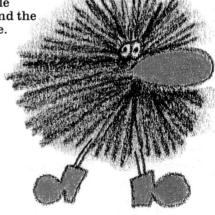

Draw the fuzzy ball body as shown above, without taking your pencil off the paper except to avoid the nose.

Smudge the ball with your finger to make it look soft. Add eyes, legs and boots.

51

Sea monsters

These monsters are all based on things that live in the sea. Find out how to draw them, colour them and do a watery background below.

You can see half a head and one evil red eye. →

Giant octopus

This giant octopus is splashing in a cloud of its own dark ink so you cannot see how big it is or where all its tentacles are. Perhaps one of them is reaching out to grab you?

Tentacles twist and curl.

Suckers.

Add white stripes if you like.

How to draw it

1. Draw the whole octopus lightly in pencil. It has a blobby head and eight coiling tentacles.

2. Mix black and blue paint and, with a brush, splash it on and around the monster, hiding parts of it.

3. When the splashes dry, paint the bits of octopus you can still see black. Add details as shown above.

Small swimmer, wearing diving suit and flippers.

Supersized sea creatures

Everyone knows that lobsters are smaller than people. But see what happens if you draw them the other way round, as here.

There are some more small sea creature shapes below. Try doing similar pictures using them.

Crab

Sea anemone

Fantastic fish

Invent a fantastic fish monster by drawing a big fish shape like this, with a huge mouth, sharp teeth, bulbous eyes and so on. Find out how to give it a slimy fish skin below.

Staring eyes

Sharp teeth

Spiky fins and tail.

Sharp shapes are scary.

Slimy fish skin

To do a slimy fish skin, first paint your fish with water or very watery colour. While it is still very wet, dab on blobs of bright paint. The blobs will smudge and blot to give mottled markings. Paint eyes and other details when the fish is dry.

Water wash

To do a water wash background as on this page, paint clean water all over your paper with a thick paintbrush. While it is still very wet, add watery blue and green paint in streaks. Let them mix and merge. Tape all four edges of the paper on to a flat surface while it dries to stop it wrinkling.

Sea serpent

This sea serpent in the seaweed is coloured with wax crayons. If you use them to do an underwater scene, you can put a water wash (see right) on top afterwards because water and wax don't mix.

Drawing the serpent

Draw a wiggly serpent in pencil.* With wax crayon, add fronds of weed. Make some go over the serpent's body and some go behind it. Colour the serpent with wax crayons, except where the weeds go over its body.

*See how to draw a snake, and other animal shapes, on pages 32-33.

Man-made monsters

If you can imagine things like a machine coming alive or a bad-tempered house, you can make monsters out of almost anything. Making something that is not alive look as if it can think or move is called anthropomorphism. See how to do it here.

Household horrors

Imagine household objects coming alive and doing things of their own accord. They may be nice, but you can make them horrible, like this cooker and vacuum cleaner.

Crazy cooker

In the box on the right is an ordinary cooker shape. On the far side of it you can see one that has been made into a cooker monster.

Cooker shape

Put eyes and teeth on the grill.

Make the cooker lean forward as if to walk.

Vac-dragon

This vacuum cleaner turns into a dragon with a snaky neck. The sucking part becomes a head with a wide mouth. Just add two evil eyes and feet with claws.

Give it feet and arms.

Flex and plug make a tail.

Kitchen shapes

Scissors

Cheese grater

Egg whisk

Here are some kitchen shapes to turn into monsters. Copy them and add eyes, arms, legs and teeth as you like.

Dark doors look like open mouths.

Bottles on step look like teeth.

Reflections in windows make eyes.

Mean streets

On a dark night, in a badly lit street, a row of houses can look menacing.* Windows turn into eyes and doors look like mouths. On the left is a particularly horrid row. The shapes are quite simple so you could try drawing your own.

Shadow spider plant

Shadows can easily become monsters. See how the plant below casts a horrible spidery shadow.*

Try it yourself. Put a plant on a table by a wall in a dark room. Shine a torch or lamp on it to make a shadow on the wall. Different plants will make different shapes.

To draw it, first do the plant and pot and colour them. Behind, put a patch of yellow and then smudge charcoal around the edges. Add the big black shadow.

Add eyes to make a monster.

Smudgy grey charcoal.

Convertible car

Here are four steps to help you convert an ordinary car into a monstrous-looking beast.

Draw one line down with three lines across it (at top, bottom and a third of the way down). Each line across is twice as long as the line above and is cut in half by the down line.

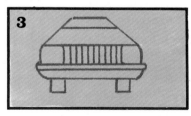

For a bumper do three lines right across below the lights. The wheels are squares below the bumper. Do lines for the grille between the lights.

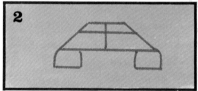

Join the ends of the lines. Do two squares for the headlights below the bottom line.

4 Adapt the shape to make your car look alive. Use curved lines. Make the lights into eyes with slit pupils. Turn the grille into fangs.

*See pages 28-29 and 67 for more eerie light effects.

Dragons

Dragons are legendary monsters that lurk in dungeons and caves. They can be friendly but many are dangerous. Here are some dragons to draw.

Fairytale dragon

Most dragons have scaly skin, wings and evil teeth and claws. Follow boxes 1 to 4 to draw a dragon. You can see how to colour it at the bottom of the page.*

1 Head and neck

Copy the picture on the left to draw the head, neck and bulging eye. Then add nostrils, the other eye and spines down the neck as shown.

2 Body and legs

Draw lines for the top and bottom of the body. Add the legs. Rub out the bits shown dotted above.

3 Wing

Draw a fan shaped wing, like in the picture. It looks like part of an umbrella, with spokes going from the bottom up to the point at the top.

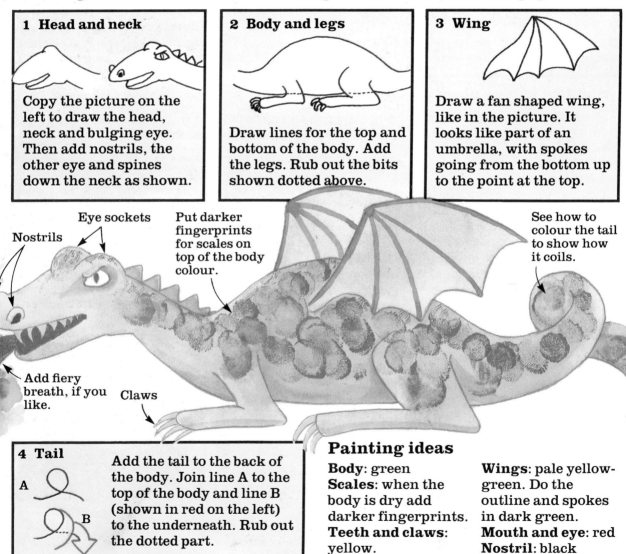

Nostrils

Eye sockets

Put darker fingerprints for scales on top of the body colour.

See how to colour the tail to show how it coils.

Add fiery breath, if you like.

Claws

4 Tail

A

B

Add the tail to the back of the body. Join line A to the top of the body and line B (shown in red on the left) to the underneath. Rub out the dotted part.

Painting ideas

Body: green
Scales: when the body is dry add darker fingerprints.
Teeth and claws: yellow.

Wings: pale yellow-green. Do the outline and spokes in dark green.
Mouth and eye: red
Nostril: black

*Or use one of the ideas for colouring dinosaurs on pages 46-47.

A dragon's lair

To make a dragon that shines in a dark lair like this one, use coloured chalks on black paper.

First draw the dragon's body. Add wings, claws, eyes and so on in contrasting colours.

For the fiery breath, draw wavy chalk lines and smudge them with a finger.

Do rocky walls in yellow. Smudge red and yellow on them to show how they are lit by the flames.

Make heaps of treasure with splodges of orange, red, green and blue.

Glowing dragon

Here is a way to make dragons that seem to glow in the dark. You need wax crayons, white paper and something pointed, like a knitting needle. Follow these steps.

1. Colour patches of bright wax crayon. Cover them with a thick layer of black crayon, as above.

2. Scratch a dragon's head into the black wax with a knitting needle*. Bright colours will glow through.

3. Your monster will shine in the blackness, like this.

*Be very careful with pointed things.

Giants, ogres and trolls

There are giants in stories from around the world. They are scary because they are so huge. Try some of the tricks shown here to help you draw them.

How to draw a giant

A whole giant is about seven times the length of his head. The circles next to this giant are the size of his head, so you can see how many head lengths different parts of his body are.

Arms reach about half way down the thighs.

1 head

Neck-waist 2 heads

Waist-knee 2 heads

Knee-foot 2 heads

You can draw people in the same way. They are seven times their head length, too. Children only measure about five of their head lengths, though.

How to make a giant look big

To show how big a giant is, put things in the picture to compare him with. In the picture below, compare the giant to the man, his dog and the trees.

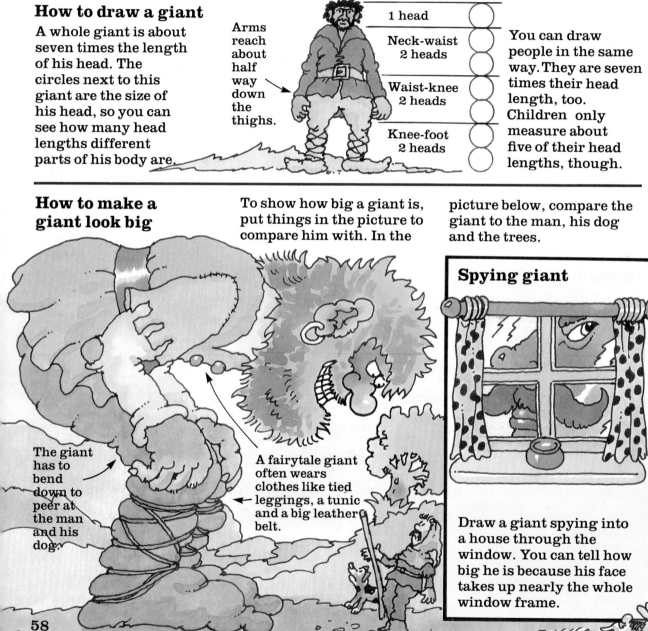

The giant has to bend down to peer at the man and his dog.

A fairytale giant often wears clothes like tied leggings, a tunic and a big leather belt.

Spying giant

Draw a giant spying into a house through the window. You can tell how big he is because his face takes up nearly the whole window frame.

When ogres look small

In this picture the boy is drawn as big as the ogre because he is nearer to you. Near things look bigger than things far away.

In the same way, the trees nearer to you are drawn bigger than those in the distance.

Compare each figure to the tree next to it to judge its true size.

The way things seem to get smaller in the distance is called perspective. You can use it to make pictures look realistic.

Castle is far away so it is drawn small.

The ogre is nearly as tall as the tree next to him.

The boy only comes a little way up the tree by him.

The bird is drawn big as it is nearest you.

Looking up at a troll

If you were standing at the feet of an enormous troll, looking up, he would look a bit like this.

Ask a grown up if you can lie on the floor and look up at them to see for yourself. Their feet look huge, while the rest of their body and head seem small.

The way the parts furthest from you look squashed up and the nearest parts seem to spread out wide is called foreshortening.*

See the hints around the picture for how to draw a troll from down below.

Make the legs and body smaller as they go up.

Do a small head with squashed up features.

His hands look big because they are nearer to you.

Draw enormous feet nearest you.

*Find out more about foreshortening on page 11.

Goblins, dwarfs and human horrors

All the creatures on these two pages have a head, two arms and two legs, like people. But these are supernatural beings that live underground, fly at night, or haunt dark dungeons.

Skeleton

This is a spooky human skeleton. It has been drawn simpler than a real skeleton, which has hundreds of bones and is very hard to draw. Follow the instructions round the picture to help you draw one yourself.

Dwarfs

Dwarfs have short bodies and legs, but big heads, hands and feet. They are usually tubby, with bushy beards.

The dwarfs in this picture are in their forge. They are quite tricky to draw. You could trace them, then try to colour them yourself. *

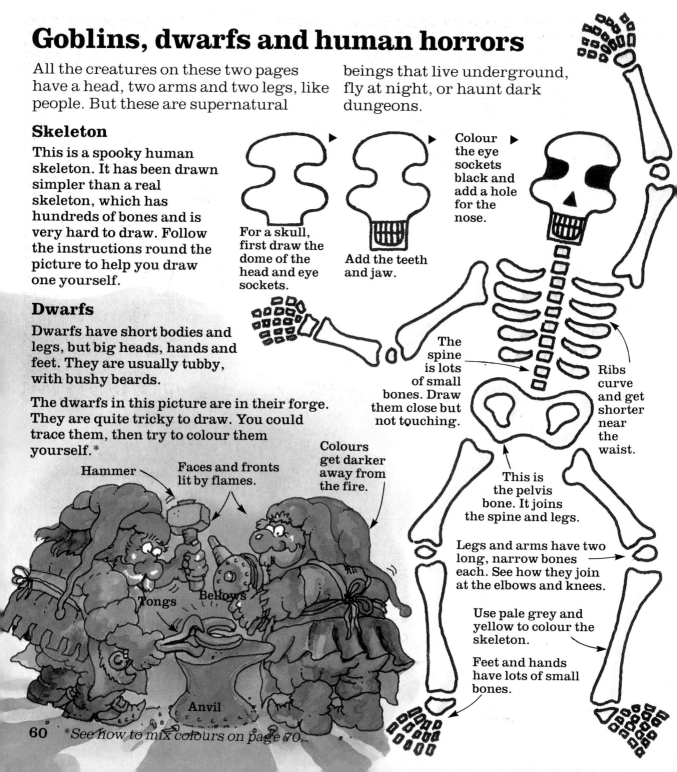

For a skull, first draw the dome of the head and eye sockets.

Add the teeth and jaw.

Colour the eye sockets black and add a hole for the nose.

The spine is lots of small bones. Draw them close but not touching.

Ribs curve and get shorter near the waist.

This is the pelvis bone. It joins the spine and legs.

Legs and arms have two long, narrow bones each. See how they join at the elbows and knees.

Use pale grey and yellow to colour the skeleton.

Feet and hands have lots of small bones.

Hammer

Faces and fronts lit by flames.

Colours get darker away from the fire.

Tongs

Bellows

Anvil

60   *See how to mix colours on page 70.

Witch's silhouette

To get the witch's shape, follow these steps.

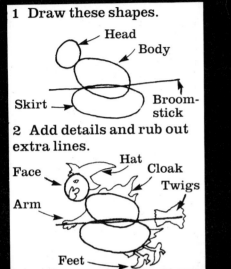

1 Draw these shapes.

Head
Body
Skirt
Broom-stick

2 Add details and rub out extra lines.

Face
Hat
Cloak
Twigs
Arm
Feet

Paint the witch black.

Draw a circle round her for the moon.

Paint outside the circle black for the night sky.

Tunnel disappears into darkness here.

Draw shoulders jutting from the side of its head so it looks as if its head is sunk low.

Do arms reaching below knees.

Drawing goblins

To draw a goblin, do a thin human shape. Give it knobbly knees and elbows and long, skinny arms. Make its head narrow with pointed ears. Colour it green with glowing eyes.

Try drawing this advancing horde of goblins in a tunnel. Put big goblins at the front of your picture and smaller ones behind. Make the tunnel floor get narrower in the distance and the walls get closer in. This is using perspective (see pages 20-21 and 59 for more about this).

61

Mythical creatures

Myths from all over the world are full of strange creatures. You may already know some of the ones shown here. Have a go at drawing them using the techniques described.

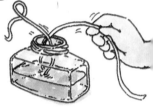

Mermaid

Mermaids are half woman and half fish. They are lovely, but dangerous. They lure sailors to wreck their ships on rocks.

To help you draw one, do a pencil guide, like this. Do a straight line to the waist and a curved line below.

Head
Shoulders
Waist
Tail

Working round the guide, draw a woman's body to the waist and a fish's tail below. Rub out unwanted lines.

Long hair
Tail

Scales on tail.

Place your mermaid on a rock in the sea and colour her like this.

Medusa

Medusa was a Greek monster. She had snakes instead of hair and anyone that looked at her was turned to stone. To draw her, first draw a horrible face. Then add snaky hair. Try printing snakes with string like this:

1. Cut some pieces of string, as long as you want the snakes to be.

2. Dip them in ink or paint and lay them in coils around the face.

3. Put a piece of scrap paper on top and press with your hand.

4. Remove the scrap paper and pick up the string. Repeat to make more prints.

5. Add eyes and forked tongues at the ends of the snaky hair.

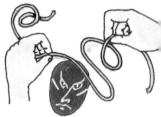

Minotaur

The Minotaur was an Ancient Greek monster with a man's body but the head and shoulders of a giant bull. Here's how you can draw him like a Greek vase painting.

Copy or trace this shape in pencil.

Cover the shape, and the rest of the paper, with orange wax crayon. The shape will still show through.

Paint black inside the shape on top of the orange. Use thick poster paint or mix powder paint and glue.*

When it is dry, scrape markings in the black with a knitting needle.

Many Ancient Greek vases are orange decorated with black figures.

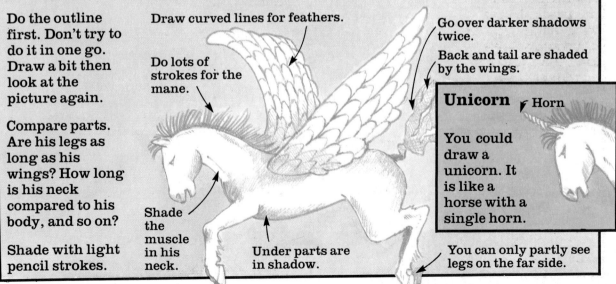

Pegasus

Pegasus was the legendary flying horse in Greek myths. Use quite a soft pencil to draw him (find out about types of pencil on page 30). The tips below should help.

Do the outline first. Don't try to do it in one go. Draw a bit then look at the picture again.

Compare parts. Are his legs as long as his wings? How long is his neck compared to his body, and so on?

Shade with light pencil strokes.

Draw curved lines for feathers.

Do lots of strokes for the mane.

Shade the muscle in his neck.

Under parts are in shadow.

Go over darker shadows twice.

Back and tail are shaded by the wings.

Unicorn   Horn

You could draw a unicorn. It is like a horse with a single horn.

You can only partly see legs on the far side.

*Or you could use black wax crayon, as on page 57.

63

Animal monsters

People have always made monsters out of animals, like the Minotaur on the previous page. Here are some more, and a game to help you make your own.

Chimaera

The mythical Greek Chimaera had a lion's head, a goat's body and a serpent's tail. Try using different drawing materials for the different parts, as explained below.

Use pencil crayons for the head. Mix strokes of brown, orange, yellow and black for the mane to make it shaggy.

Chalk is good for the hairy goat's body. Smudge brown chalk all over, then use charcoal for details and shading.

Smudge shadow under legs.

Legs shaggy at the top.

Use felt tips on the serpent's tail for contrast. Use two shades of green and put black scales on top.

Do hooves and outline black.

Make ripples by colouring with corrugated cardboard under your paper.

Tail

Do as many humps as you like. Make them smaller as they go away from you.

Loch Ness monster

Legend says that a monster lives in Loch Ness in Scotland. This is what it is traditionally supposed to look like.

Shapes to draw

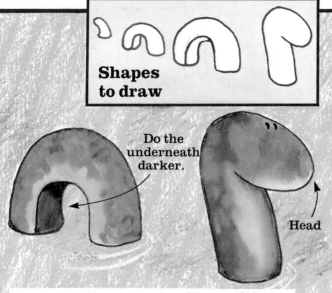

Do the underneath darker.

Head

Use a pencil to draw the shapes of the monster, shown in the box above. Colour them greeny-black. For the water, do patches of green and blue wax crayon. Lay the crayons on their sides and rub.

Animal monsters game

Make your own strange animal monsters by playing this game.

Draw a head at the top of a sheet of paper. It can be a real animal's head, or an imaginary one. Fold the paper so only the end of the neck can be seen.

Pass it to a friend, who adds a body. Fold again so just the end of the body is seen.

Pass the paper on. Someone else adds legs. Unfold the paper to see your creation.

King Kong

King Kong is quite modern, but is already legendary. Try drawing this picture starring him.

Draw the skyscrapers. It is as if you are above them so you can see their roofs. They get narrower as they stretch away from you towards the street below.

Draw the giant gorilla emerging from behind the buildings.* He is dark, but paler underneath where he is lit from the street. Make it night to add atmosphere.

Clouds and moon.

Small plane for King Kong to grab.

*See pages 58-59 for some ways to make him look big.

People or monsters?

All the monsters on these two pages are people of a kind - or at least, they might be.

He seems to blend into the snow.

Yeti

Yetis live in the Himalayas. Nobody knows if they are a type of person, ape or monster. Draw this one on blue paper.or paint a blue background.

Paint a shaggy Yeti with white paint on a brush. Use as little water as possible so the paint is quite dry and goes on in rough streaks. Add a blizzard whirling round him.

Werewolf

This ordinary man turns into a werewolf on nights with a full moon. Colour him with pencil crayons. Use light layers of brown, yellow and pink for skin, and shades of brown for hair.

As he changes, it is as if his face is pulled forward: make his nose longer and his chin stick out; give him a thinner, longer mouth; do his ear pointed and higher up; make him sprout hair on chin, cheeks and forehead.

Fully changed, he is like a fierce wolf. Draw a wolf's muzzle. Add sharp teeth and glowing red eyes. His ears are now on top of his head. He is hairy all over.

You can make a blizzard by spraying white paint from a toothbrush, as on page 57.

Frankenstein's monster

Frankenstein stitched together a sort of man and brought him to life artificially. He escaped and terrorized the neighbourhood. This is a portrait of him.

This picture is lit from above. The shadows are black blocks. Copy the shapes in pencil then colour them black. Practise drawing faces like this from newspaper pictures. They often look like blocks of light and shadow.

← Lit from above, there are deep shadows in the eye sockets and under the nose, lower lip and chin.

Portrait of a vampire

Vampires rise from the dead and drink human blood. Draw the famous vampire, Count Dracula, like this:

Draw his head and cloak and colour them with crayons. He has red eyes, fangs and a ghastly green skin. Do eerie black face shadows as shown.

Do a shadow behind Dracula, the same shape, only bigger. Use paint or felt tip so it is blacker than he is.

Try copying the two small Dracula figures on the right and add shadows to match.

Eerie light experiment

To see the dramatic shadows that light can cast on your face, try this:

Sit in a dark room in front of a mirror and shine a torch from different angles on to your face.

Compare the shadows you see in the mirror with those in the pictures below. They are most dramatic when the light shines from over your head or below your chin. Also note how the shadow of your body is cast on the wall behind you.*

Lit from below, the shadows are on the upper lip, cheekbones and forehead.

*See more special effects on pages 28-29.

Mechanical monsters

On these two pages are ways to draw robots and other machine-like monsters.

Destructobot

This destructobot is quite hard to draw. Try using a grid to help, like this:

Draw a grid of squares in pencil, as at the bottom of this page. Do the squares as big as you like.

Look at the squares one at a time. Copy the shapes in each one on to the same square in your grid. Then rub out the grid lines.

The labels round the picture show you some details.

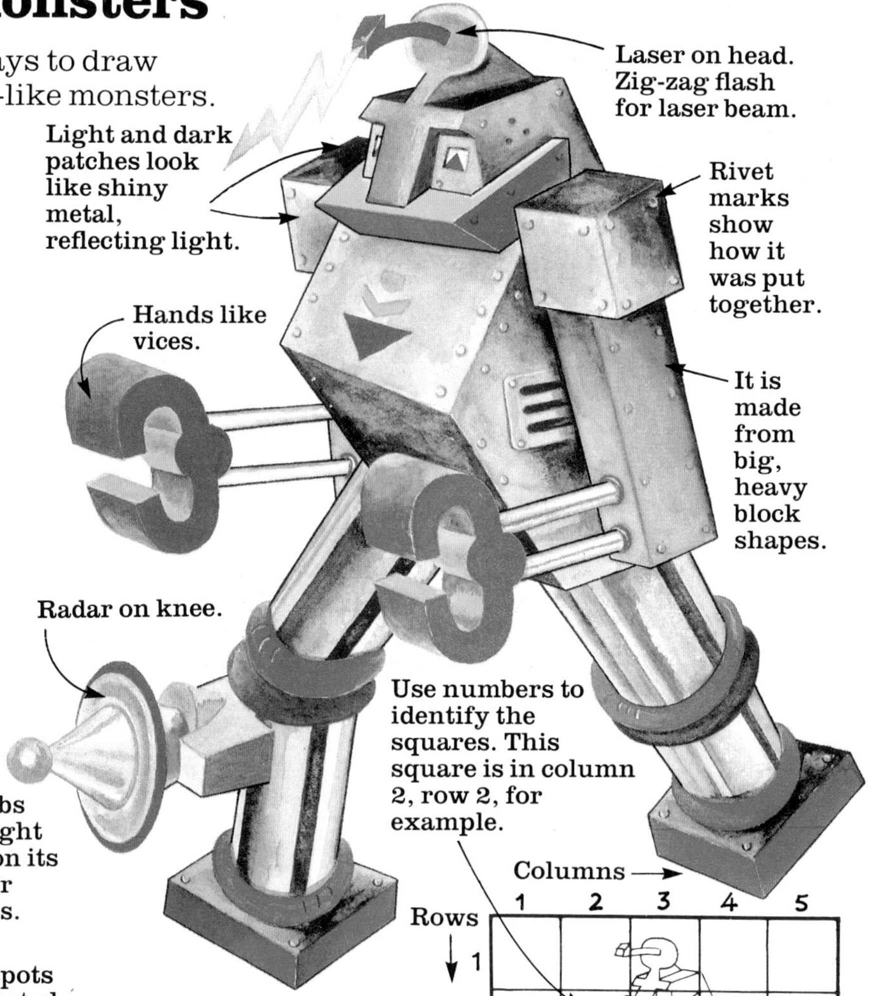

Laser on head. Zig-zag flash for laser beam.

Light and dark patches look like shiny metal, reflecting light.

Rivet marks show how it was put together.

Hands like vices.

It is made from big, heavy block shapes.

Radar on knee.

Use numbers to identify the squares. This square is in column 2, row 2, for example.

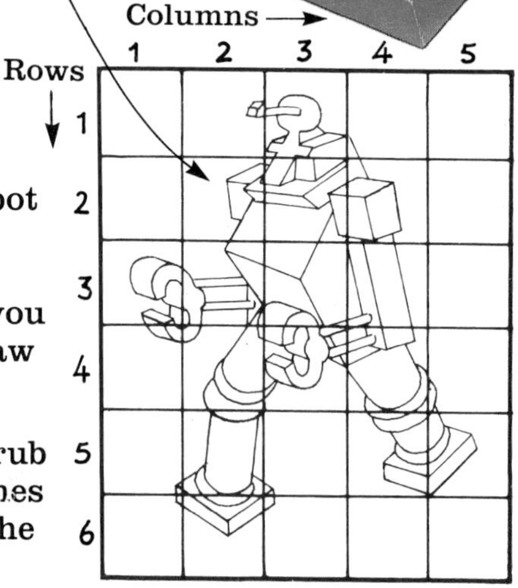

Rogue robot

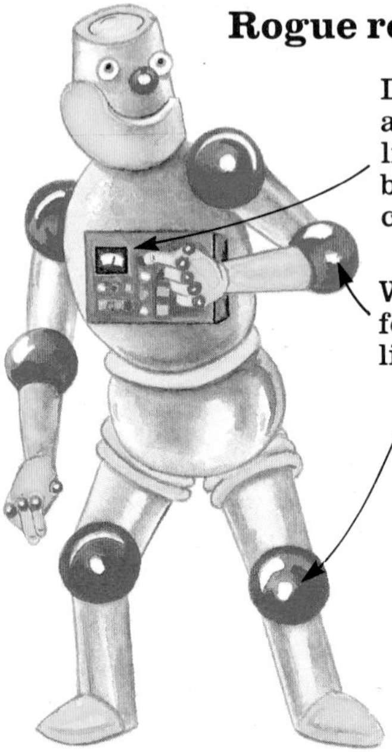

Do knobs and bright lights on its body for controls.

White spots for reflected light.

◀ You can draw this robot from circle shapes joined together. The small picture shows you the shapes to use. Draw them in pencil first.

Before you colour it, rub out the parts of the lines that are not there in the big picture.

Columns →

Rows	1	2	3	4	5
1					
2					
3					
4					
5					
6					

Put a grid on tracing paper over other monsters in this book to help copy them.

Machine mixer

This monster is made from parts of machines. Try to draw a similar one and shade it with dots and lines.

Use dots on rounded parts. The closer the dots, the darker the shadows.

Use lines on flat bits. Criss-cross lines make darker shadows.

Shading lines (called hatching).

Criss-cross lines (called cross-hatching).

Earth digger.

Hydraulic arm.

Dots work well on rounded shapes. This is called stippling.

Radar dish.

Caterpillar tracks.

Darkest parts are solid black.

Computer monster

To turn a computer into a monster*, draw it with lights flashing, parts flying and wires escaping. Putting people in the picture adds to the fun.

Chips

Screen

Cassette

This flex has swept a boy off his feet.

Print-out paper

Keyboard

If you have a computer at home or at school, use it as a model.

This boy is trying to pull the plug out.

*See more ways to make machines look like monsters on pages 54-55.

69

Techniques and materials

Here is a round up of all the techniques and materials in this part. The chart on the right has a column for each material telling you how you can use it. A white panel across more than one column refers to all the materials in those columns.

Red

Red and yellow make orange.

Yellow
Blue

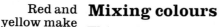

Blue and red make purple.

Yellow and blue make green.

Mix red, yellow and blue to make brown.

Mixing colours

This colour monster shows you which colours mix to make other colours. You only need red, yellow and blue to make all these colours. (Felt tips do not mix like this). Use black to make them darker and white to make them paler.

The pencil family

Pencils can be hard or soft. Soft pencils make thick, fuzzy lines. Hard pencils make thin, clear lines. Most pencils are marked with a code to tell you how hard or soft they are. See how the code works on the right.

2H H HB B 2B

Harder: up to 9H
Softer: up to 9B.

Most ordinary pencils to write with are HB.

Using fixative sprays

Fixative sprays stop pictures in soft materials like charcoal, chalk and soft pencil smudging. They come in aerosol cans and you can get them from art suppliers. Never breathe the spray or work near a flame. It is best to use them outside, since they smell very strong. Do not throw empty cans on a fire.

Pencil crayons

Pencil crayons are good for doing hairy effects (see pages 64 and 66).

Pencils

You probably use pencils the most. You can draw with them first even if you colour afterwards.

Drawing lines

Use the point of crayons, pencils or charcoal pencils for fine lines and the side of the point for fuzzy lines and shading.

Shading with lines and dots

You can shade areas with lines and dots. See an example of this on page 69.

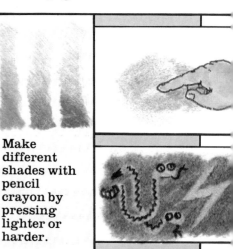

Make different shades with pencil crayon by pressing lighter or harder.

Textures

Make textures by rubbing over things placed under your paper (see pages 47 and 64).

Charcoal	Chalk	Wax crayons	Paint	Ink	Felt tips

Shading

Lie a stick of charcoal, chalk or a wax crayon on its side and rub. Snap the sticks to make them smaller if you need to.

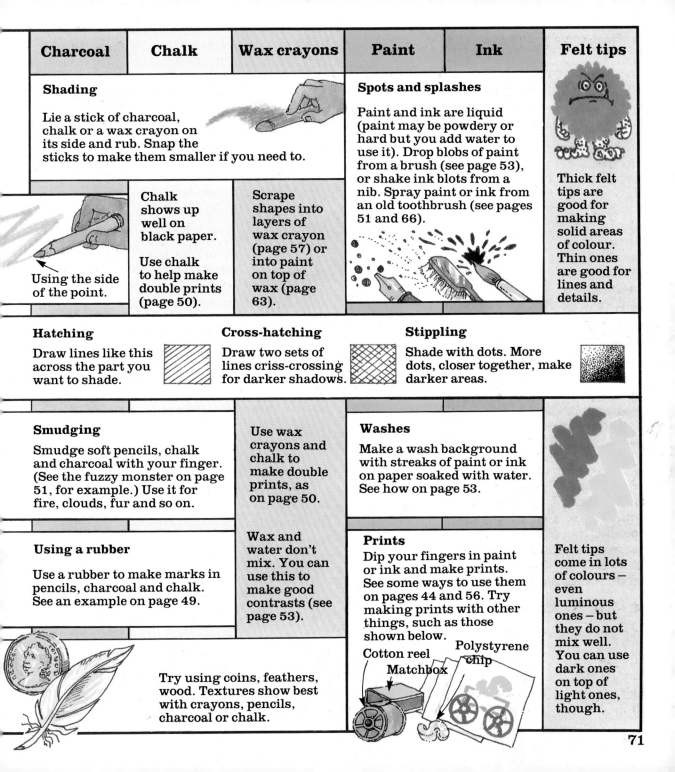

Using the side of the point.

Chalk shows up well on black paper.

Use chalk to help make double prints (page 50).

Scrape shapes into layers of wax crayon (page 57) or into paint on top of wax (page 63).

Spots and splashes

Paint and ink are liquid (paint may be powdery or hard but you add water to use it). Drop blobs of paint from a brush (see page 53), or shake ink blots from a nib. Spray paint or ink from an old toothbrush (see pages 51 and 66).

Thick felt tips are good for making solid areas of colour. Thin ones are good for lines and details.

Hatching

Draw lines like this across the part you want to shade.

Cross-hatching

Draw two sets of lines criss-crossing for darker shadows.

Stippling

Shade with dots. More dots, closer together, make darker areas.

Smudging

Smudge soft pencils, chalk and charcoal with your finger. (See the fuzzy monster on page 51, for example.) Use it for fire, clouds, fur and so on.

Use wax crayons and chalk to make double prints, as on page 50.

Washes

Make a wash background with streaks of paint or ink on paper soaked with water. See how on page 53.

Using a rubber

Use a rubber to make marks in pencils, charcoal and chalk. See an example on page 49.

Wax and water don't mix. You can use this to make good contrasts (see page 53).

Prints

Dip your fingers in paint or ink and make prints. See some ways to use them on pages 44 and 56. Try making prints with other things, such as those shown below.

Cotton reel

Matchbox

Polystyrene chip

Felt tips come in lots of colours – even luminous ones – but they do not mix well. You can use dark ones on top of light ones, though.

Try using coins, feathers, wood. Textures show best with crayons, pencils, charcoal or chalk.

Monster facts

Throughout this book you will have seen how to draw many monsters, both imaginary and based on real animals or people. Here is some more information about monsters around the world. You can draw them by using shapes already in the book.

Cyclops

In Greek legend the Cyclops were a tribe of fierce giants who lived on the island of Sicily. They had only one eye, in the middle of the forehead. They were supposed to be extremely strong and lived for a very long time.

To draw a Cyclops you could adapt the giant shape on pages 58-59.

Bigfoot

There are many stories about yetis being seen in the Himalayan mountains. There are also reports of a similar monster in North America. It is called 'Bigfoot' or 'Sasquatch'. Bigfoot is thought to be 2m (7ft) tall and to leave 40cm (16in) long footprints.

Use the ideas for the yeti on page 66 to draw Bigfoot.

Lake monsters

On pages 64-65 you can see how to draw the Loch Ness monster. Many other lakes around the world also claim to have similar monsters, such as Slimey Slim (USA), Hvaler Serpent (Norway) and Pooka (Ireland).

Kraken

The word 'Kraken' means 'sea monster'. For hundreds of years there have been reports of huge monsters shaped like giant squid, which appeared out of the sea and killed sailors.

You could make up your own Kraken using these ideas and those on page 52.

Giant birds

Giant birds appear in many legends. The Roc in the Arabian story 'Sinbad the sailor' was supposed to be a huge bird with long, curved talons. It was strong enough to kill an elephant.

You can find out how to draw many other animal monsters on pages 64-65.

Grendel

The monster Grendel lived in Denmark near the royal castle. The King liked music and dancing but Grendel hated such sounds. He attacked the castle and killed many of those inside.

Base your drawing of Grendel on the werewolf picture on page 66. Make it bigger and fiercer, with lots of shaggy hair.

Part 3
HOW TO DRAW
ANIMALS

Anita Ganeri and Judy Tatchell

Designed by Steve Page

Illustrated by Claire Wright

Cartoon illustrations by Jon Sayer

Additional illustrations by Rosalind Hewitt

Contents

About part three

Animals may be elegant, cuddly, fierce or exotic. Some are easier to draw than others.

Cartoon pictures usually have a simple outline with exaggerated features.

Big ears

Large beak

Big eyes

If you like animals, you will probably enjoy drawing them. Drawing animals will also help to improve your general drawing skills. This part shows you how to draw and colour all kinds of animals in easy step-by-step stages.

Some animals make good cartoons. Their natural characteristics can be exaggerated to make them look funny. Throughout this part there are suggestions for animals which make particularly good cartoons and how to draw and colour them.

Professional tips

Throughout this part, there are tips from professional animal illustrators to help you. Here are a couple to start with.

It is easier to draw an animal if you can look at one at the same time but this is not always possible. Animal illustrators often draw from photographs instead of live animals.

Take a sketchbook with you if you visit a farm or a zoo. Sketch details, such as a head or a leg, as well as whole animals.

Picture coloured with crayons and watercolours.

Cartoon coloured in with felt tips.

Pencil sketch

If you want to draw realistic animals, this part will help you to get the shapes right. You can see how to draw fur, slimy skin, wrinkly hide and so on.

All you need to start drawing is a pencil and paper but there are lots of suggestions throughout this part for further materials to use.

Using simple shapes

Animals' bodies look complicated but they are mostly made up of quite simple shapes. In this part you can see how to draw animals using simple shapes and building up the outline around them. Here are some examples.

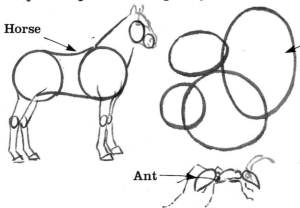

Horse

Ant

Squirrel

The shapes used to draw these animals are made up of rough circles, egg shapes, curves and lines.

Here you can see how the outlines of the animals have been built up around the starting shapes.

A horse's head

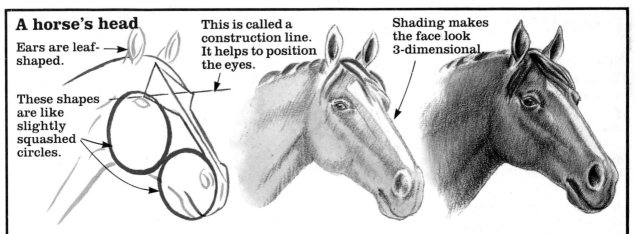

Ears are leaf-shaped.

These shapes are like slightly squashed circles.

This is called a construction line. It helps to position the eyes.

Shading makes the face look 3-dimensional.

Try copying the shapes above to draw a horse's head – first the red, then the blue, then the green ones. Draw the lines in faint pencil.

Draw in the outline around the shapes and add more details to the eyes and nose. Sketch in the mane. Colour the horse and then add some shading.

You can use watercolour paints or crayons to colour the horse. This one was coloured in reddish and dark brown crayons over a pale brown watercolour base.

Colouring in

Animals have different types of skin depending on where and how they live. They may have fur to keep them warm or patterned skin for camouflage. Here, you can find out how to use different drawing materials to show fur, skin, hair and so on. The ideas will help you to colour in the animals in this part.

Furry coats

Smooth wash.

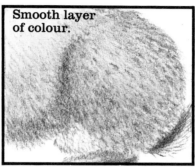

Smooth layer of colour.

Using watercolour paints, start with a smooth wash of a pale colour. Let it dry. Add short strokes of richer and darker colour for fur.

If you are using crayons, start with a smooth layer of pale colour. Build up the brighter and darker hairs on top, using short strokes.

For black and white pictures, use the side of a soft pencil, such as a 3B*. Use a sharper, harder pencil, such as a 3H*, to add more detail.

Hairy coats

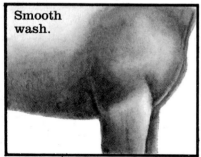

Smooth wash.

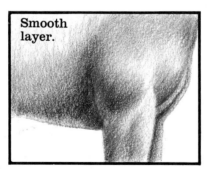

Smooth layer.

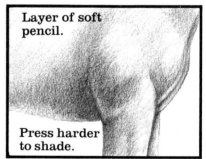

Layer of soft pencil.

Press harder to shade.

For smooth hair, do a flat wash. Put the main colour on top, leaving pale areas for shine. Use a thicker mix of colour or a darker shade for shadows.

With crayons, you can keep the texture smooth by using blunt ones. Leave some streaks for shine. Go over shadowed areas again, or use a darker shade.

For black and white pictures, you need a smoother finish than for furry coats. Use a soft pencil, with a harder pencil for the outline.

Skin

Watercolour wash.

Colours blend at the edges on damp paper.

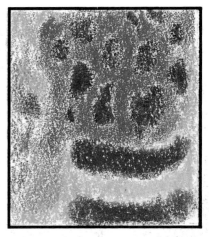

For a brightly coloured skin, such as a snakeskin, sketch the pattern in light pencil. Then colour the pattern in paint or crayon.

For a mottled skin, like a frog, use blunt crayons for a soft finish. With paint, add different shades while the paper is still damp.

Wax crayons are useful for drawing bright skins as they give a shiny finish. It is harder to get fine detail with wax crayons, though.

Colouring cartoons

You can colour cartoons in bright, flat colours. The detail is in the outline of the cartoon and you don't need to shade them.

Professional tip

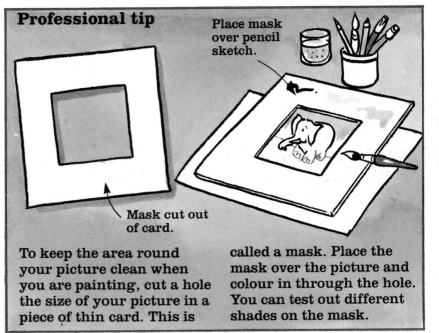

Place mask over pencil sketch.

Mask cut out of card.

To keep the area round your picture clean when you are painting, cut a hole the size of your picture in a piece of thin card. This is called a mask. Place the mask over the picture and colour in through the hole. You can test out different shades on the mask.

Cats and dogs

The main feature of a cat's body is its very flexible spine. A dog's spine is straighter. Here are some cats and dogs to practise. Can you see the differences?

A cat

Sketch the markings in pencil before you colour them.

Rub out unnecessary lines before colouring.

Sketch the shapes above in pencil. Start with the shapes shown in red, then the blue ones, then the green. Don't worry if you cannot get them right at first. Just keep trying.

Smooth off and refine the outline. Add details such as eyes, a nose and whiskers. Begin to colour the cat starting with the palest colour and building the darker markings on top.

For a marmalade cat use orange, yellow and brown. You could use watercolour for the base and crayon for the fur. Do some streaks of grey to show the fur on the white front and paws.

A dog

The body is leaner than a cat's.

Feathery streaks round the outline make it shaggy.

Putting shadow underneath makes the dog look as if it is standing on the ground.

The starting shapes for a dog are similar to those of a cat but the proportions are slightly different. The nose is longer and the body is less rounded.

The dog's chest is deeper than a cat's. Its underside tapers up towards the back legs. You can see how the tail is really an extension of the backbone.

This is an English Setter. Start with a pale grey, then build up darker streaks and markings on top. Finally, add some white streaks to highlight the long hair.

Comparing cats and dogs

Here you can see how the shapes of cats and dogs differ when they are sitting or lying.

A cat's back is curved when it is sitting. It is curled almost into a circle when it is lying down.

It is easier to draw an animal from the side than from the front.

The dog's back is much straighter than the cat's when it is sitting or lying down.

Cartoon cats and dogs

Cartoon cats and dogs are easier to draw than real ones. Sketch your cartoon in pencil, then go over the outline in black felt pen. Colour the cartoon in bright, flat colours.

Puppies and kittens have more rounded bodies than adult cats and dogs.

Horses

Horses are quite difficult to draw. Try the method below. Start with simple shapes using a light pencil until the body is right. Then you can colour it in.

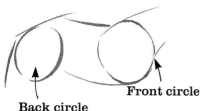

Back circle

Front circle

Draw two circles, one slightly bigger than the other. The larger circle is the front of the horse and the smaller one the back. Join them with curved lines to form the body.

Head

Neck

Rounded knee joints.

Extend the larger circle with two tapering lines for the neck. Draw a narrow diamond shape for the front of the head. Draw the tops of the legs with small ovals for the joints.

Construction lines on head.

Weight line. (See bottom of opposite page.)

Add the ears, lower legs and the hooves. The green shapes will help you to draw the head. Pencil in construction lines* to position the eyes and nose. You can rub them out later.

Long pencil strokes for mane and tail.

Now you can start to add more details to the basic shapes. Do the tail and mane in long pencil strokes. Draw the eye, nostril and mouth and rub out the construction lines.

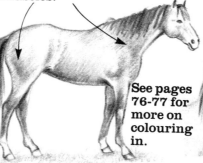

Shading to show muscles.

See pages 76-77 for more on colouring in.

Show where the horse's muscles are with light shading. Shade underneath the body, too. This makes the animal look more rounded and solid (or 3-dimensional).

Main colour

Dark shading

Build up the horse's main colour using soft crayon strokes. Leave some white patches for highlights. Use a darker shade of the main colour to finish off the shading.

See page 75 for more about construction lines.

Horses in motion

Walking

Head held low.

A front leg is lifted and the opposite back leg is the furthest behind.

Trotting

The head and legs are lifted higher than in a walk. Opposite legs come forward together.

Cantering

The head is stretched out. Opposite legs are flung out in front and behind.

A cartoon horse

Follow the stages below to draw a cartoon horse. Start with block shapes and sticks to get the proportions of the body looking right.

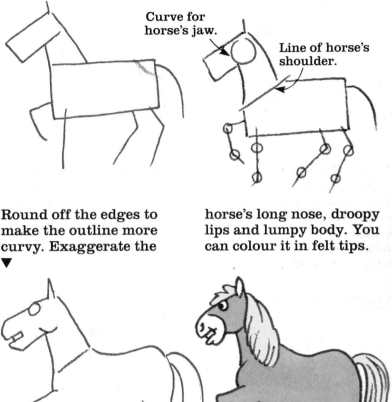

Curve for horse's jaw.

Line of horse's shoulder.

Round off the edges to make the outline more curvy. Exaggerate the ▼ horse's long nose, droopy lips and lumpy body. You can colour it in felt tips.

Professional tip

When you are drawing an animal, it can help to draw a construction line which shows where the animal's weight is falling. This helps you to work out how to position the legs and makes the picture look balanced.

Farm animals

On these two pages you can see how to draw farm animals and how to turn some of them into cartoons. If you live near a farm, try sketching the live animals. You could practise the ones here first, to get the idea of the shapes.

A cow

Watercolour paint was used here.

Shallower body.

The head is more rounded.

Long, slender legs.

Weight line*

To draw a cow, pencil in the red, blue and green shapes. It has a heavier body and a shorter neck than a horse. Its neck and spine form a straighter line.

Shade the sandy brown areas. Then do the bluey black patches. When it is dry, go over the darker areas with more bluey black paint.

Use similar basic shapes for a calf but make them smaller. A calf's legs are longer in relation to its body than a cow's. Its body and limbs are more slender.

A cartoon sheep

Egg-shaped head.

These lambs' legs are furrier than the sheep's.

Some pale blue shading makes the sheep look more fluffy.

To draw a cartoon sheep, copy the shapes above. The body is made up of three rounded shapes. Draw sticks to show where the legs go.

Draw a curly outline round the sheep's body to show its woolly coat. Draw in ears and give the face a lazy, sleepy look. Block in the shapes of the legs.

Cartoon lambs are a similar shape to sheep but have longer necks and legs. To make cartoons look more professional, go over the outline with black felt tip.

Cartoon ducks and pigs

You can base a cartoon duck shape on triangles and ovals. Build up the feathery outline around them.

Triangles for tail and feet.

Pigs make good cartoons because it is easy to exaggerate their round, lumbering bodies.

Start with three round shapes.

Triangular ears.

Ragged tail feathers.

Snout

Ripples show how the duck is moving.

Fat legs

Cloven hooves

A hen

The hen was coloured in a pale brown watercolour wash. The darker patches were then built up on top.

Weight line*

Start with the red circles. Then draw the hen's back, shown in blue. Then add the other blue lines and the head.

A cockerel

Use contrasting colours for the feathers.

Weight line*

This shape is quite tricky to draw.

Use long curves for the cockerel's body. It has a bigger comb than the hen and more dramatic colouring.

*The weight line is explained on page 81.

83

Countryside creatures

On these pages you can see how to draw a few of the animals that live in the countryside. They are all shy creatures, but some, such as the fox and squirrel, also venture into towns.

Rabbits

This curve helps to position the other back foot.

Soft, furry outline.

Thin arms and big paws.

A rabbit's body looks soft and rounded. Start with the two red circles. Then add the curve for the back.

Colour the rabbit pale yellowy brown. Use short strokes of grey for fur. Add some white strokes to make it fluffy.

Rabbits have lots of features which you can exaggerate to make a cartoon. Start by drawing the shapes above.

Exaggerate the rabbit's long, floppy ears, its buck teeth and big feet. Give it a cheerful, smiling face.

A stag

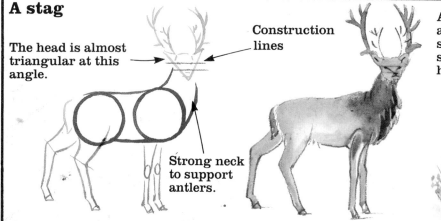

The head is almost triangular at this angle.

Construction lines

Strong neck to support antlers.

A deer is smaller and more slender than this stag. Only stags have antlers.

The basic shapes for a stag are similar to those for a horse, as shown in red above. It holds its head higher, though, and has a strong neck.

Draw the outline round the shapes. Use construction lines to position features on the head. Put down the base colour on the body, with some shading.

Add areas of richer reddish brown. Then add dark brown shadows under the body and neck. The antlers are grey with highlights to make them look velvety.

Cartoon hedgehogs

A cartoon squirrel

Start with the shapes below for a cartoon squirrel. Then give it round cheeks full of nuts, large front teeth and a bushy tail.

To do a cartoon hedgehog, exaggerate its pointed nose and prickles. Start with an egg shape with a circle at the front, as shown.

You could add stripes to make it look like a chipmunk.

A fawn

It has a more rounded head than a stag.

A fawn is shorter, has a less muscular neck and longer, thinner legs in relation to its body than a stag.

Start with a light wash and build the darker colours on top. Add the white dapples when the paint is dry.

A cartoon fox

This cartoon fox has a wily expression due to its long, pointed nose and hooded eyes. To draw a real fox, you can use the same shapes as for a dog (see pages 78-79).

Big cats

All cats have the same basic shape. They have long, streamlined bodies and flexible spines. Look for differences in their head shapes and their markings.

A tiger

The shapes for this tiger are adapted from the cat shape on page 6. Start with the red shapes, then the blue, then the green ones.

Draw the outline of the tiger round the shapes. It has lumpier shoulders and a less rounded head than a domestic cat.

To colour it in, start with the lighter colour and build up the markings on top. See the box opposite for more about markings.

Heads

Big cats' heads differ more than their bodies. Draw the outlines and construction lines in faint pencil.

The tiger looks like a heavier version of a domestic cat, with a broad face.

Lions have long, heavy faces and chins. Only males have golden manes.

The cheetah has a small, neat head to make its body more streamlined.

The jaguar has round ears. Its mouth and nose form a pear shape.

Cartoon big cats

Lines to help position features.

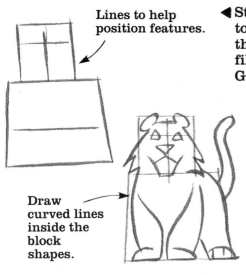

Draw curved lines inside the block shapes.

Tiger

◀ Start off with block shapes to draw this tiger. Use them as guidelines for filling in the body shapes. Give it a furry head.

The stripes help to show the contours of the body.

Lion

The eyes go above this line.

These triangles show how the limbs are positioned.

Use triangular shapes as a basis for this lion's body, with a circle for the head.

Its hooded eyes give it a superior expression.

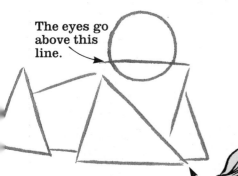

Markings

Watercolour paint was used for these examples. You could also use soft crayons.

Tiger's stripes added on top of a slightly damp, flat wash.

Hairs in lion's mane added in a richer colour on a flat wash.

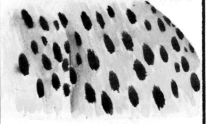

Cheetah has spots evenly spaced all over body.

Jaguar's markings in rosettes with spots in the middle.

Jungle animals

Here you can see how to draw some animals that live in the jungle. If you go to a zoo, try sketching the animals.

Look at how they move and at their expressions. These details will help to make your pictures more realistic.

A gibbon

A gibbon is a type of monkey.

Gibbons have long arms and strong hands and feet to help them grip branches. To draw a gibbon, start with these shapes.

Start to colour the gibbon's fur using pale yellowy brown. Make the outline fuzzy using short strokes of a darker colour.

Refine the picture by shading and adding more definition to the fur. Add detail to the face, making the features quite sharp.

A gorilla

The gorilla has longer fur than a gibbon.

Gorillas are similar to gibbons, but their bodies and limbs are thicker and heavier. Draw the gorilla's squat shape. Colour it in black and white to show the highlights on its fur.

An orang-utan

This orang-utan is made up of rounded shapes. It has powerful shoulders like the gorilla and a large, broad face. Its head is set low on its shoulders. Colour the long, shaggy fur in shades of orangey brown.

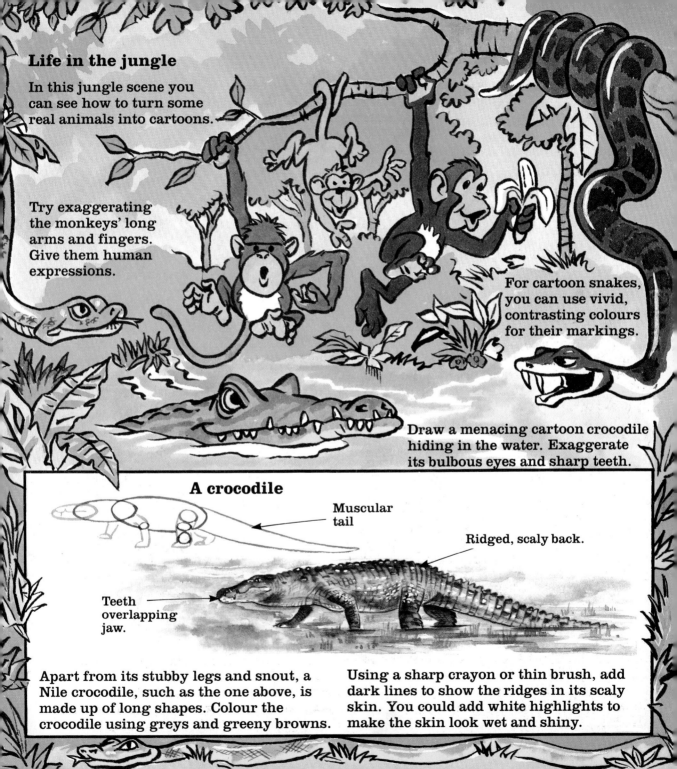

Life in the jungle

In this jungle scene you can see how to turn some real animals into cartoons.

Try exaggerating the monkeys' long arms and fingers. Give them human expressions.

For cartoon snakes, you can use vivid, contrasting colours for their markings.

Draw a menacing cartoon crocodile hiding in the water. Exaggerate its bulbous eyes and sharp teeth.

A crocodile

Muscular tail

Ridged, scaly back.

Teeth overlapping jaw.

Apart from its stubby legs and snout, a Nile crocodile, such as the one above, is made up of long shapes. Colour the crocodile using greys and greeny browns.

Using a sharp crayon or thin brush, add dark lines to show the ridges in its scaly skin. You could add white highlights to make the skin look wet and shiny.

Desert animals

Many animals that live in the desert have special features which help them to survive in hot, dry conditions.

A camel

> The head is held almost horizontally.

A Bactrian camel has two humps. A dromedary has one.

The camel stores fat in its hump to insulate it against the heat. Follow the red, blue and green lines to draw the basic shape.

The Bactrian camel has long fur on its neck.

Paint the camel with an even yellowish brown wash. While the paper is still damp, dab on areas of reddish and dark brown.

A cartoon camel

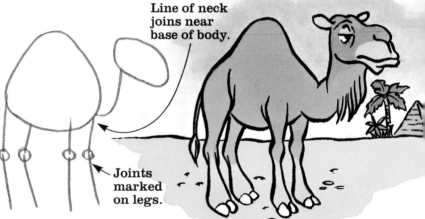

Line of neck joins near base of body.

Joints marked on legs.

For a cartoon camel, exaggerate the size of the head and the knobbly knees. Do the outline in pencil first.

Give the camel large, droopy lips. Half-closed eyes make it look haughty. Give it some shaggy fur round its hump and neck.

Snakes and lizards

Some reptiles' bright skins warn off predators. Others are coloured to blend in with their surroundings. Try to work out the basic shapes for yourself.

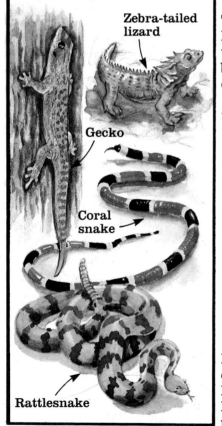

Zebra-tailed lizard

Gecko

Coral snake

Rattlesnake

Small animals

Small, furry animals usually have rounded bodies. You can adapt the mouse shape on the right to draw hamsters and guinea pigs.

A mouse

◀ To colour the mouse, paint a sandy brown wash over it. Leave it to dry and then use a darker brown pencil to draw short strokes for the fur.

Beady black eyes.

A guinea pig

▲

A guinea pig is made up of chunkier shapes than the mouse. This one is a long-haired variety. Sketch faint lines showing how the hair should lie before you paint it.

A hamster

A hamster is larger and rounder than a mouse. Paint it with a watery light brown. When it is dry, paint strokes of fur in a stronger mix of the same colour. Then do the darker areas on top.

▼

A cartoon mouse

A mouse makes a good cartoon because you can exaggerate its big ears and nose and its long tail. See if you can work out the basic shapes for this mouse yourself.

More wild animals

Here are some real and cartoon pictures of several wild animals. They all have different shapes and so will give you good drawing practice.

A kangaroo

Use very watery white paint for the highlights.

A cartoon kangaroo

Movement lines

The kangaroo's weight is centred over its back legs. It uses its heavy tail for balance.

After you have painted the body reddish brown, add white highlights and dark shadows.

To draw a cartoon kangaroo, you can exaggerate its huge feet, short arms and big nose. Draw movement lines to show that it is bounding along. This kangaroo has a baby in its pouch enjoying the ride.

A cartoon aardvark

A zebra

An aardvark's strange but simple shape makes it a good cartoon. This one has a long snout and big ears.

A zebra has a similar shape to the horse on **page 80**. Its body is slightly shorter, though, and it has a very short mane.

All zebras are stripy but the patterns can differ. Use a pencil to sketch in the markings on your zebra's coat.

Giraffes

A giraffe has plenty ▶ of features which you can exaggerate for a cartoon. Its body is a funny shape with a long neck, small head and stumpy horns.

To draw a real giraffe, start with the rough triangular shape shown in red. Then add the shapes for the legs and head.

▼

See the box below for a hint on how to colour in the giraffe's markings.

Colour the zebra in using paints or crayons. A zebra's stripes provide it with camouflage behind long stalks of grass so that from a distance it is hidden from hunting lions.

Professional tip

When using watercolour paints for an animal's markings, try wetting the paper first with clean water. Paint the colour on while it is still damp. The different areas of colour will merge together at the edges, giving a softer impression.

Big animals

You can practise drawing tough, wrinkled hides on the elephant and hippo on these pages.

Many big animals also make good cartoons because of their lumbering, heavy shapes.

An elephant

This African elephant has larger ears than an Indian elephant.

Start with the shapes above – first the red shapes, then the blue ones and then the green ones.

Paint the elephant with a grey watercolour wash. Keeping the paper damp, dab on some sandy brown patches and darker grey shadows. When it is dry, add the wrinkles. Alternatively you could use crayons. Keep the base colours smooth and use a sharp crayon for the wrinkles.

A cartoon rhino

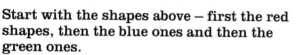

Horns Ears

The steps above will help you to draw a cartoon rhino. For the body, start with four overlapping ovals (egg shapes).

Add sticks to show where the legs go. Then mark in the positions of the horns and ears, as shown in pencil above.

You can then draw in the eyes, mouth, legs and tail. Go over the outline in black felt tip and then colour the rhino in.

A cartoon elephant

A cartoon whale

A cartoon elephant looks like a simplified version of a real one. You could make your elephant look almost human by drawing it reading a newspaper or dancing, like the one above.

Start with the shape shown in red to draw a cartoon whale. Draw the whale half-submerged in the sea, squirting water out of its blow-hole. Draw its tail fins jutting out from below the surface.

A hippopotamus

Add the wrinkles and colour the features when the rest of the colours are dry.

A cartoon hippo

The hippo is a similar shape to the elephant, but it has a squatter body and stubbier legs. It holds its head down low.

Paint washes of grey and pinky brown. Blend the edges by dipping a brush in water and "feathering" the colours together.

Try drawing a cartoon based on the shapes for the real hippo. Emphasize its jaw and make its legs shorter and fatter.

95

Bears

Here you can see how to draw three famous types of bear. Look at pages 76-77 for some hints on colouring in fur.

A brown bear

Some brown bears stand up to 2.5m tall on their hind legs. They are a similar shape to polar bears. This bear was coloured with light brown, reddish brown and dark brown crayon.

A polar bear

The polar bear is one of the strongest animals in the world. Its rounded body is covered in thick fur.

Shade the body with pale yellow and bluey grey to make it stand out on white paper.

A cartoon panda

You can use a panda's vivid markings to make a striking cartoon. Pandas eat bamboo, so you could draw it surrounded by shoots.

Cuddly animals

Small, furry animals look cuddly because of their size and softness. These ones are made up of rounded shapes.

Koala bears

This koala bear, with its baby on its back, is climbing a eucalyptus tree. Draw the shapes for the mother first and then position the baby.

Bluey black and brown watercolours were used here for a soft effect.

Keep the paper damp so the colours blend.

A baby loris

White dots in the eyes make them look shiny.

A baby loris has big brown eyes and a furry coat. Draw a faint outline so that when you colour it in there are no hard edges. Use long strokes of a darker colour to make it look fluffy.

A seal cub

Draw the seal's body and head shape first, and then position the flippers. Seal cubs have soft, furry white coats. They lose the fur as they get older.

Chicks

Chicks have big feet compared to their bodies. Colour them rich yellow, then use orangey brown to shade them and to define the fluffy feathers.

97

Creepy crawlies

Many people find creepy crawlies repulsive. Some have beautiful details on their bodies, though, such as fine veins on their wings, or coloured markings.

Spiders

This is a garden spider.

A spider's body is made up of ovals with lines for the legs, as shown by the coloured shapes over to the right.

This spider was painted in watercolours. Start with a pale wash and build up the darker shades on top. Leave a white cross on its back.

You could draw a huge tarantula hanging from its web. Exaggerate its hairy legs, bulging eyes and round body.

An ant

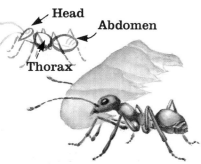

Head

Abdomen

Thorax

All insects' bodies are divided into three parts, called the head, thorax and abdomen. Draw the rough shapes for an ant and colour them as shown.

A wasp

All insects have six legs which join on to the thorax.

Tiny veins in wings.

A wasp's body is a similar shape to an ant's but its head and abdomen are more curved. It has delicate wings. Its vivid colours warn off enemies.

Bees

Bees have fatter, rounder bodies and smaller wings than wasps. They are covered in tiny hairs. Try a cartoon bee as well as a real one.

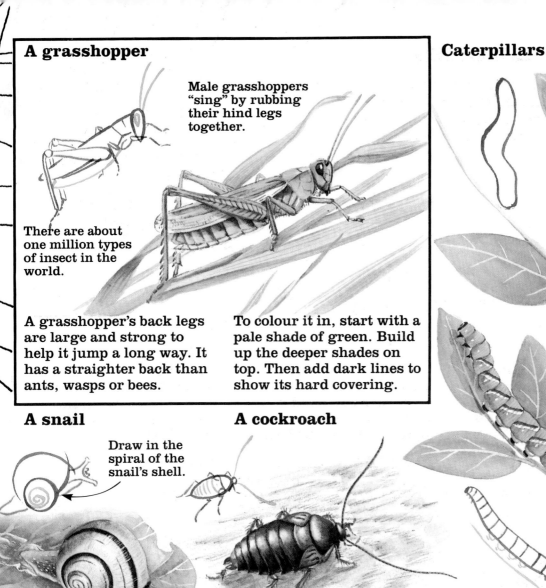

A grasshopper

Male grasshoppers "sing" by rubbing their hind legs together.

There are about one million types of insect in the world.

A grasshopper's back legs are large and strong to help it jump a long way. It has a straighter back than ants, wasps or bees.

To colour it in, start with a pale shade of green. Build up the deeper shades on top. Then add dark lines to show its hard covering.

Caterpillars

Caterpillars are made up of lots of segments which get narrower towards the head. This one has bright streaks to warn off predators.

Long, hairy caterpillars make good cartoons.

A snail

Draw in the spiral of the snail's shell.

The white streaks on the snail's shell make it look hard and shiny. Draw a glistening trail of slime behind the snail.

A cockroach

A cockroach has a hard, shiny black or brown covering, so make it shiny. Draw fine hairs on its legs and give it long antennae.

Animals that swim

Here you can see how to draw some animals which live in or near water. Fish have simple shapes but you can colour them brightly. You can also try more complicated creatures such as penguins, seahorses and turtles.

A shark

To draw this cartoon shark, start with the outline above. Sharks have sleek, streamlined bodies to help them move quickly through the water. Draw the fin jutting out above the water.

Gills

Position the other fins and the gills. Draw a curve in the tail. The top part is longer and narrower than the bottom part. The shark's sharp, triangular teeth slope backwards.

More cartoon fish

These tropical fish show variations on the fish shape and some ideas for colour. Give them exotic fins and tails.

An octopus

Try copying this giant octopus resting on the sea bed. It has an egg-shaped head and eight legs covered in suckers.

▼

Penguins

To draw realistic penguins, use the shapes shown on the right. Their bodies are smooth and streamlined. Their small flippers make them look comical. To draw the icy water, do blue watercolour streaks. Then dip your brush in water and "feather" the colour out.

Add eyes when paint is dry.

Pale shading on bodies.

A turtle

Watercolour on body.

Delicate crayoning on head and fins.

A turtle's shape is made up of an oval for the body and leaf shapes for the flippers and head. The shell looks like armour-plating.

A seahorse

A seahorse has an S-shaped body and very fine fins. Highlight the ridges on its body with white paint.

Frogs

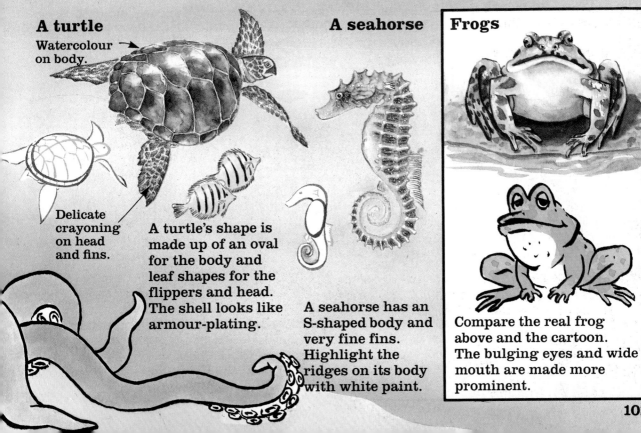

Compare the real frog above and the cartoon. The bulging eyes and wide mouth are made more prominent.

Animals that fly

All the animals on these two pages can fly but their body and wing shapes differ widely. Some of them have beautiful markings which are fun to colour in.

Birds

Head, body and tail form a straight line.

These are the basic shapes for a tern. Look at other birds to see how their shapes differ.

The tern is white except for its head, beak and feet. Shade its body with a pale bluey grey.

You can adapt the shapes to do birds in other positions. Remember that the wings grow out

from the bird's spine. They always bend in the same place and curve slightly backwards.

Feathers

Feather shapes in brown watercolour.

Details added in crayon.

Practise drawing a bird's wing in close up. Use short strokes of coloured crayon or paint to show the detail on the feathers.

An owl

Heart shapes for the body and head.

This owl was coloured with dabs of reddish and dark brown paint on damp paper. Paler strokes show its downy breast.

A flamingo

The flamingo's beak, neck and body form a rough S-shape. Colour it in shades of pink, using pale blue for the shadows.

A cartoon toucan

Draw rough shapes in pencil for the beak and body until the proportions look right. Then refine the outline.

You could colour it in any shades you like.

Butterflies

Pastels give a powdery look.

To draw butterflies in different positions, copy the red shape on paper and cut it out. Fold it to the position you want, then look at it as you draw. These were coloured in artist's pastels.

A peacock

Use a very thin brush for the feathers.

Detail of "eye".

Start the peacock by drawing a large oval on its side, in light pencil. Then draw a body in the middle and colour the feathers.

Cartoon bats

For this scene, copy or trace these bat silhouettes. Colour them in black wax crayon, then go over them in a dark blue watercolour wash.

Using watercolour: advanced tips

Many of the realistic pictures in this book are done in watercolour paint. Basic watercolour techniques are quite simple but you may need a bit of practice to achieve the special effects below.

On this page there are some extra tips on using watercolour and on the types of paper you can use.

Building up colour

When you use watercolour, remember to build up the colours gradually.

Sketch out the basic shapes, then paint on a pale wash of a base colour.

Let the wash dry, then add other colours on top. You might use different shades of your base colour. Several thin layers of the same colour gives a smoother finish than one thick layer of a darker colour.

Then add highlights and shading. Highlights give texture; for example, the shine on a snail's shell. Use white paint for highlights, letting the colour underneath dry first. Shading in a darker colour helps show muscles and define features.

Special effects

Here are some of the different effects you can get using watercolour.

If you paint on to dry paper, the colours will be quite strong and definite.

To avoid hard edges, wet the paper first with clean water and paint the colour on whilst it is still damp. The colours will merge to give a softer look.

'Feathering' is another technique for avoiding harsh lines. Dip your brush in clean water and brush the edges of the colours gently so the lines blur.

To get a mottled effect paint dabs of watery paint next to each other while the paper is still damp. The colours will streak together.

Paper

For sketching you can use any type of paper. The best paper to use, though, is an unlined paper without a shiny surface.

Cartridge paper is very good for painting on. Professional artists use different sorts of cartridge paper depending on what effect they want.

Paper comes in different colours and in different 'weights'. Heavier paper is good for watercolour work as it takes paint well and does not wrinkle as it dries out.

Some artists prefer to use a slightly creamy-coloured paper for watercolour work as it shows up delicate colouring better than pure white paper.

Professional tip

Some paper stretches as it gets wet and then shrinks as it dries, causing it to wrinkle. Professional artists sometimes 'stretch' their paper before using it to prevent this happening. They wet the sheet of paper first and then lay it out carefully on a board to dry. All four sides are stuck down firmly with tape so that the paper lies absolutely flat. As it dries, it does not wrinkle so it can be painted on easily.

Part 4
HOW TO DRAW
MACHINES

Moira Butterfield
and Anita Ganeri

Designed by Kim Blundell and Robert Walster

Illustrated by Kim Blundell, Chris Lyon, Steve Cross, Peter Bull and Graham Round

Additional designs by Steve Page

Contents

About part four

If you are interested in machines you may enjoy drawing them. This part shows you techniques for drawing all kinds of machines.

You can find out how to draw realistic pictures of machines you see around you, such as cars, trains, planes and bikes.

There are also tips on drawing cartoon machines – making them look funny and friendly, or fierce and frightening.

You can use your imagination to invent fantasy machines such as robots and spaceships. There are lots of ideas to start you off.

At the end of this part, there is a section on designing machines, using professional techniques such as "cutaways".

Drawing tips

Before you start drawing, here is some information about different drawing materials. You can find out how to use them, for instance to shade an object to make it look solid.

For sketching practice and for experimenting, you can draw on pieces of scrap paper. For more finished drawings you many want to use cartridge paper which is better quality.

Materials and shading

Paints, inks and thick felt tips give flat areas of colour. These are good for simple pictures and diagrams. Use a darker colour to do the shading.

This shape is on page 108

Copying pictures

Here is a method you can use to copy a picture. This helps you to work out how it was drawn.

Use a ruler to measure out the grid.

You could use this method to copy pictures in this part.

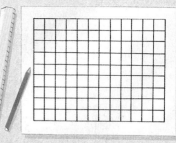

1 On tracing paper, draw a grid made up of equal-sized squares, like the one shown above. Make the grid large enough to cover the whole picture.

Pencils, crayons and fine felt tips give a clear outline. You can use them for hatching – a way of shading using lines.

Use straight lines to shade flat surfaces and curved lines for rounded surfaces.

Crossed lines, called cross-hatching, are used to give darker shading. This technique works well on flat surfaces.

This shape is on page 122.

This shape is on page 115.

A useful method for shading curved surfaces is to use lots of dots. This is called stippling. Use pencils, crayons or fine felt tips. The closer together the dots, the darker the shading.

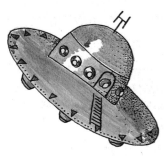

This shape is on page 126.

Charcoal and chalk can be used for big pictures. You can shade by smudging the lines with your finger. You can also smudge a soft lead pencil.

This shape is on page 116.

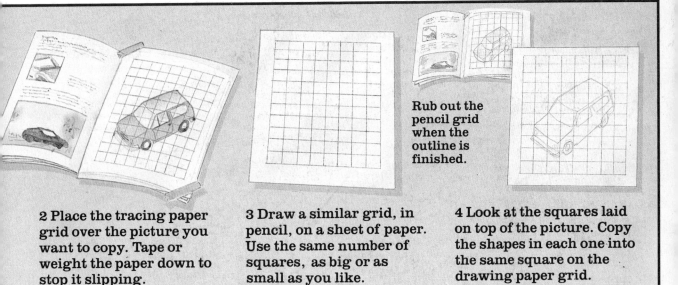

Rub out the pencil grid when the outline is finished.

2 Place the tracing paper grid over the picture you want to copy. Tape or weight the paper down to stop it slipping.

3 Draw a similar grid, in pencil, on a sheet of paper. Use the same number of squares, as big or as small as you like.

4 Look at the squares laid on top of the picture. Copy the shapes in each one into the same square on the drawing paper grid.

Cars

Cars are made up of simple shapes and are quite easy to draw. You can make them look sleek and shiny, or you can draw cartoon cars with human faces.

There are some suggestions for car pictures on the next four pages. Looking at a real car, or a photo of one, will help you to get the shapes right.

A car shape

The lines shown in pink should be parallel*.

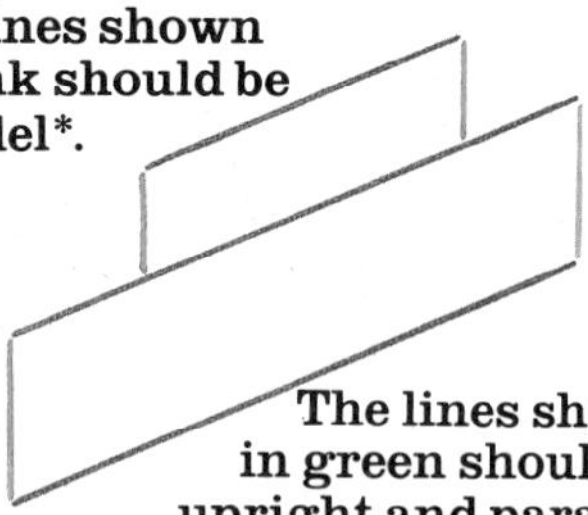

Draw a car shape inside the boxes.

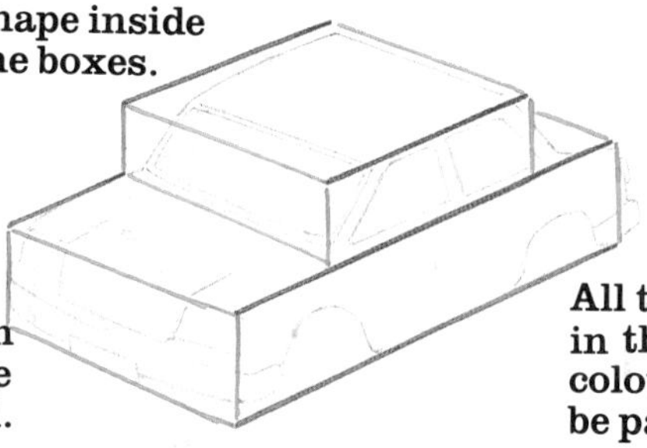

The lines shown in green should be upright and parallel.

All the lines in the same colour should be parallel.

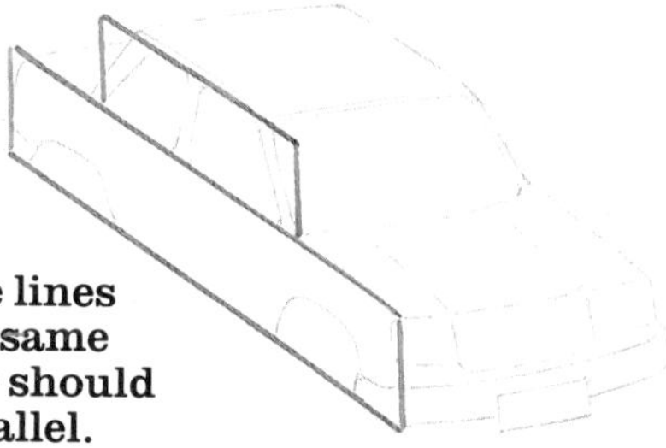

To draw an angled view of a car, pencil in two slanting boxes like the ones above. You can rub them out later.

Add sides to the boxes to give a more solid shape. Use the boxes to help you work out the outline of your car.

If you want to vary the angle of the car, change the angle of the two boxes you begin with.

Colouring in

Once you have drawn the car shape you can colour it in and finish it off as shown here.

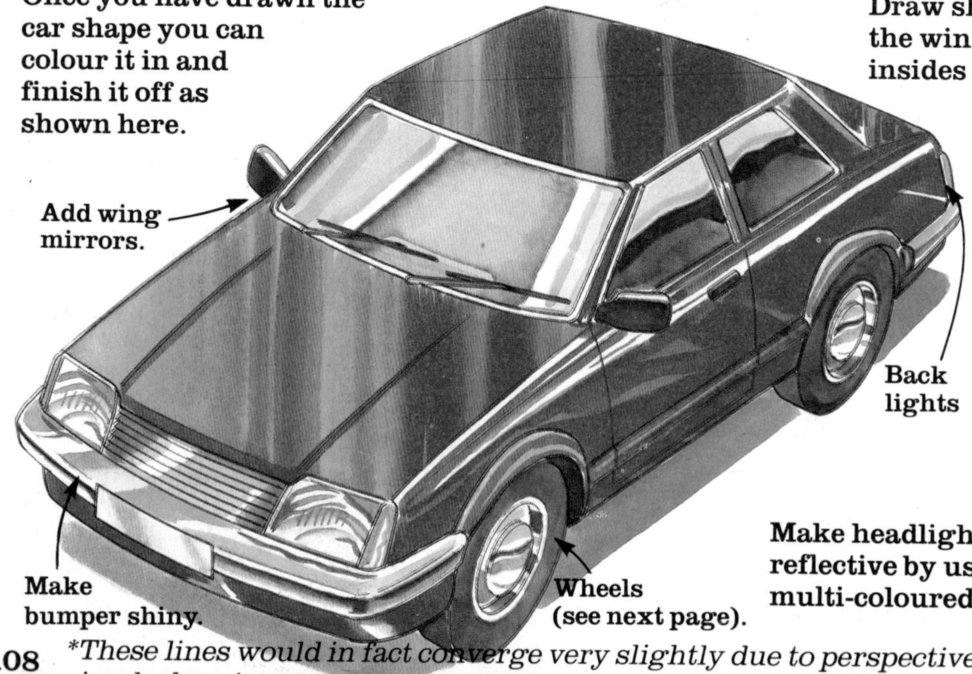

Draw shadowy shapes in the windows to suggest the insides of the car.

To make the paintwork shiny, use streaks of light and dark colour. White streaks give a polished look.

Add wing mirrors.

Back lights

Make bumper shiny.

Wheels (see next page).

Make headlights look reflective by using multi-coloured flashes.

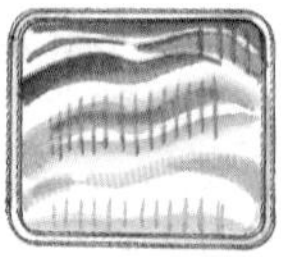

*These lines would in fact converge very slightly due to perspective but for this simple drawing you can draw them parallel, see page 117 for more on perspective

Drawing a wheel

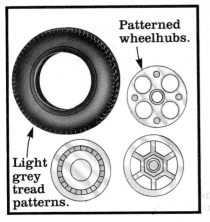

Patterned wheelhubs.

Light grey tread patterns.

Draw a curve to show the inside edge of the wheelhub.

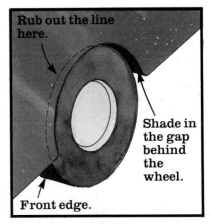

Rub out the line here.

Shade in the gap behind the wheel.

Front edge.

You can make a car tyre look rounded and full of air by using grey shading, as above. Add a light grey treadpattern and a wheelhub.

To show a wheel at an angle, draw an oval shape on the side of the car body, and draw in a smaller oval for the wheelhub.

Rub out the part of the oval that goes over the car body. Draw in the front edge of the wheel, and shade it in.

Custom cars

Some people "customize" cars as a hobby. That means they add their own special decorations to make totally original vehicles. On the right are some suggestions for you to copy or trace.

Wing mirrors

Blobmobile

Flaming speedster

Zebra Mark 1

Flower power

Sports car

Sports cars have a streamlined shape, to help them go faster. You can get this effect by starting with the shape on the right.

Wedge-shaped front

Sloping back

This car has been done in three shades of the same colour. The background and road are blurred to show speed.

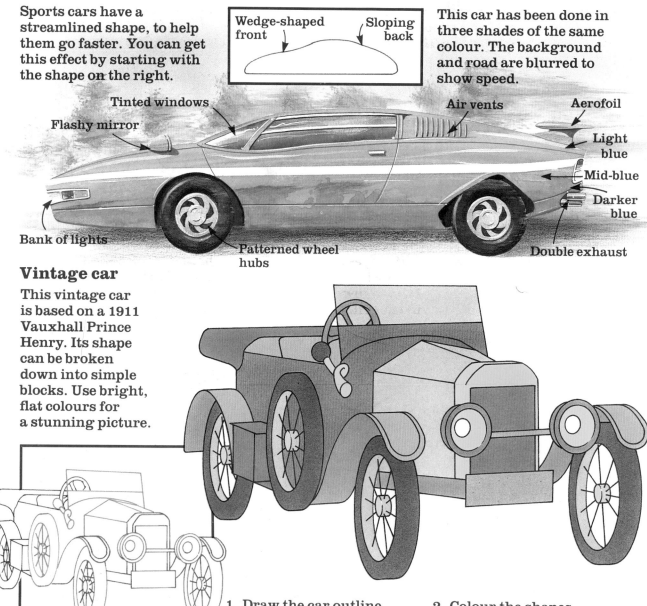

Tinted windows

Flashy mirror

Air vents

Aerofoil

Light blue

Mid-blue

Darker blue

Bank of lights

Patterned wheel hubs

Double exhaust

Vintage car

This vintage car is based on a 1911 Vauxhall Prince Henry. Its shape can be broken down into simple blocks. Use bright, flat colours for a stunning picture.

1 Draw the car outline, copying the lines on the left – the red ones, the green ones, then the blue ones.

2 Colour the shapes brightly. You could outline each shape in black to make it stand out.

Cartoon cars

You can give cars different characters when you draw them as cartoons. Use car parts, such as headlights or the grille to give the car human features such as eyes, mouths and eyebrows. There are some examples of how to do this below.

Draw a friendly car with a round, bright body and wheels bending inwards. You could use the grille as a smiling mouth, the badge as a nose, and the headlights as eyes.

This fierce car has a square, sharp-cornered body and big wheels. Add narrow, shifty eyes and use the front wings as eyebrows. Draw a row of sharp teeth in the grille.

Draw a worn-out car with a dented body, flat tyres, a cracked window and battered paintwork. Make the grille into a sad mouth and turn the headlights into droopy, tired eyes.

Fast and slow

This car looks as if it is speeding round a bend in the road. Draw all the body lines curved, and add curved speed lines to show that the car is moving very fast.

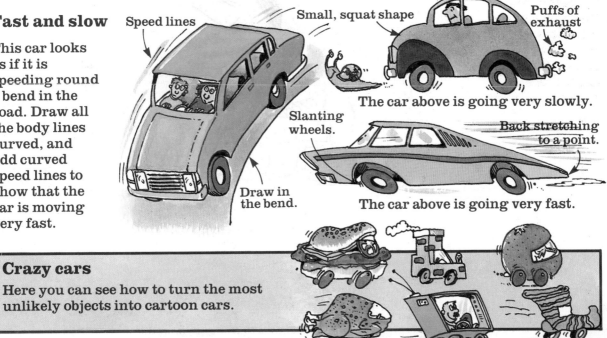

Speed lines

Small, squat shape

Puffs of exhaust

The car above is going very slowly.

Slanting wheels.

Draw in the bend.

Back stretching to a point.

The car above is going very fast.

Crazy cars

Here you can see how to turn the most unlikely objects into cartoon cars.

Big vehicles

On these two pages you can find out how to draw different types of big vehicles such as trucks, tractors and diggers. These are fun to draw because they are made up of big, solid shapes, and you can use bold, bright colours.

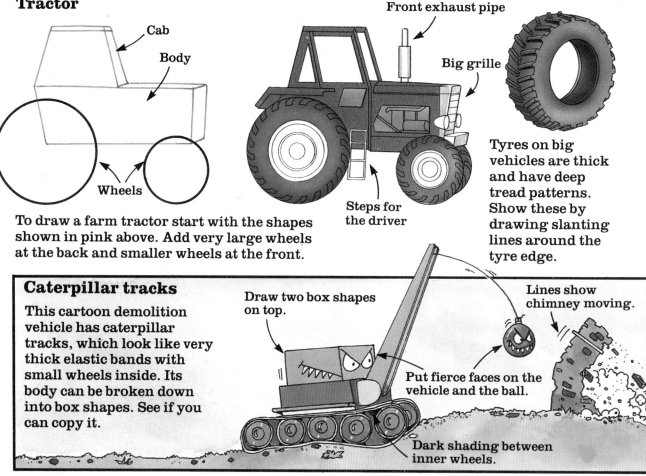

Tractor

Cab

Body

Wheels

To draw a farm tractor start with the shapes shown in pink above. Add very large wheels at the back and smaller wheels at the front.

Front exhaust pipe

Big grille

Steps for the driver

Tyres on big vehicles are thick and have deep tread patterns. Show these by drawing slanting lines around the tyre edge.

Caterpillar tracks

This cartoon demolition vehicle has caterpillar tracks, which look like very thick elastic bands with small wheels inside. Its body can be broken down into box shapes. See if you can copy it.

Draw two box shapes on top.

Lines show chimney moving.

Put fierce faces on the vehicle and the ball.

Dark shading between inner wheels.

Convoy

You could make a long wall frieze based on the vehicles in the convoy on the right. Copy them freehand, or use a grid to enlarge them as shown on pages 106-107. You could add cars (pages 108-111), motorbikes and bicycles (pages 120-121) to the convoy if you like.

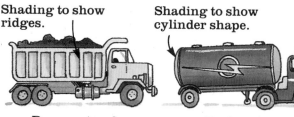

Shading to show ridges.

Shading to show cylinder shape.

Dumper truck

Tanker

Sunset scene

The steps below show you how to draw a scene of a tractor working in a field at sunset. Do the drawing on a large piece of paper. You could use a black felt tip for the outlines in the picture and then colour them in with paints or inks.

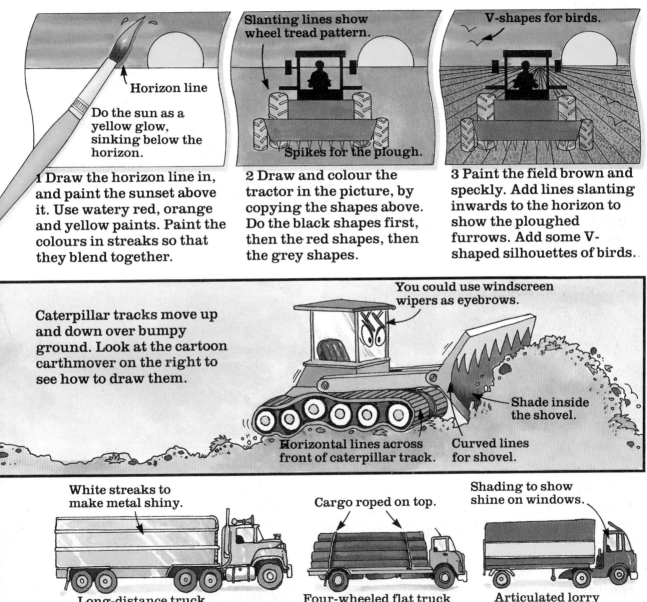

Horizon line

Do the sun as a yellow glow, sinking below the horizon.

1 Draw the horizon line in, and paint the sunset above it. Use watery red, orange and yellow paints. Paint the colours in streaks so that they blend together.

Slanting lines show wheel tread pattern.

Spikes for the plough.

2 Draw and colour the tractor in the picture, by copying the shapes above. Do the black shapes first, then the red shapes, then the grey shapes.

V-shapes for birds.

3 Paint the field brown and speckly. Add lines slanting inwards to the horizon to show the ploughed furrows. Add some V-shaped silhouettes of birds.

Caterpillar tracks move up and down over bumpy ground. Look at the cartoon carthmover on the right to see how to draw them.

You could use windscreen wipers as eyebrows.

Shade inside the shovel.

Horizontal lines across front of caterpillar track.

Curved lines for shovel.

White streaks to make metal shiny.

Long-distance truck

Cargo roped on top.

Four-wheeled flat truck

Shading to show shine on windows.

Articulated lorry

113

Ships and boats

Here you can see how to draw ships and boats, building them up from simple shapes. There are also some colouring techniques for you to experiment with.

Ship shapes

The shape of an object appears to change, depending on where you are standing when you look at it. This position is called your viewpoint. The horizon is generally level with your viewpoint. Here are some ships seen from different angles.

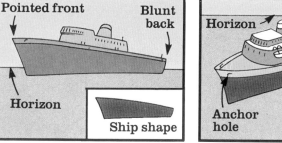

To show you are level with the ship, put the horizon line halfway up the picture.

Put the horizon line near the top to show you are looking down on the ship.

To show you are looking up at the ship, put the horizon line low.

Night lights

Use wax crayons and blue paint for this cruise liner.

1 Draw the outline in yellow wax on white paper. Put yellow and red reflections in front of the ship.

2 Add portholes along the side of the ship, and some strings of yellow lights.

3 Paint over the whole picture with dark blue paint. It will not stick to the wax, and your ship drawing will show through.

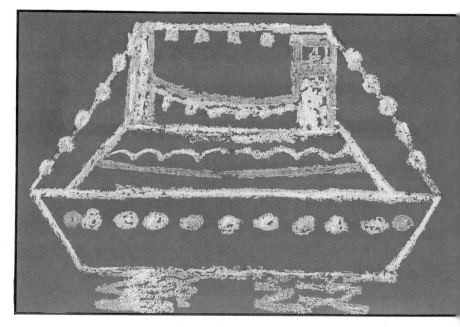

Racing yacht

This racing yacht is done in a sketchy style. Use sharp pencil crayons to scribble on the colours.

1 Draw the yacht outline in faint crayon to start with, copying the shape shown in the box on the right.

2 Scribble in the mast and sail. Scribble stripes on the sails and some people shapes on deck.

3 Go over the hull shape with crayon, missing out the lines behind the sails. Use green and white crayons to scribble in sea.

This crayon style gives the impression of speed and seaspray.

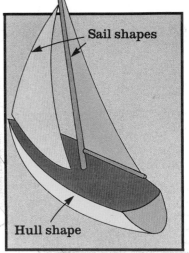

Sail shapes

Hull shape

Sea splashing outwards.

White crayon and bright colours on sails.

Darker colours on hull.

Sea cartoons

Submarine and galleon shapes make good cartoons, as shown below.

Sub periscope

Add cartoon fish and waves.

Draw someone climbing out of the sub hatch.

Rows of sails

Shield-shaped back

Cannon on sides

Galleon shape

Draw a wrecked ship covered in weeds.

Add a treasure chest.

Snake sea monster

115

Trains

Trains make striking pictures because of their chunky shapes. Here you can see how to draw old-fashioned steam trains and modern high-speed models.

Steam trains

To do a steam train shape, ▶ begin by drawing a cylinder in pencil. Start with an oval and then add two lines and a curve, as shown on the right. Add some wheels at an angle, and join them together with rods. You can then add other extras such as a funnel, buffers, tracks and a driver's cab. Use felt tips for bright, flat colours.

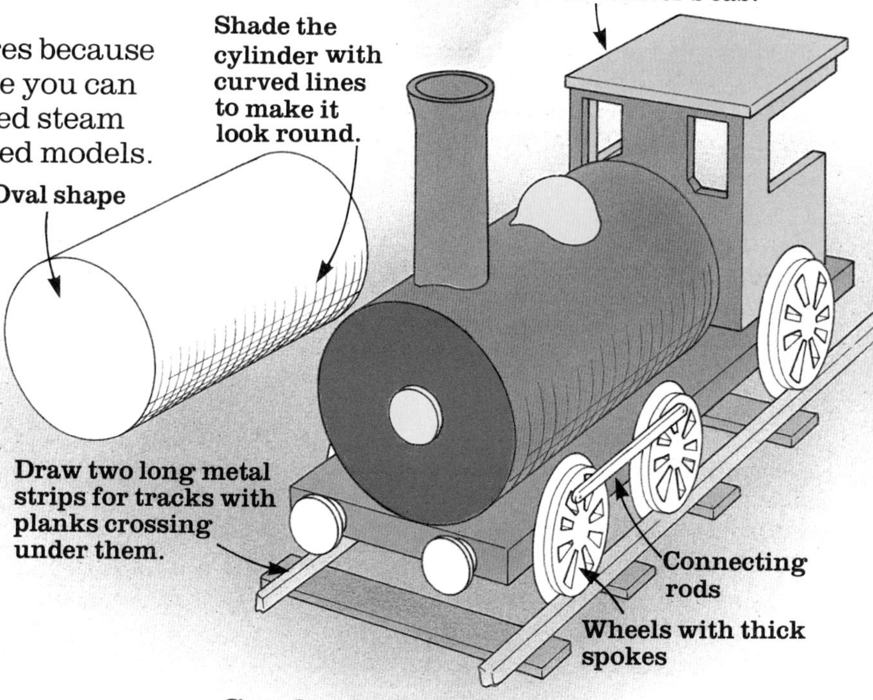

Shade the cylinder with curved lines to make it look round.

Use a box shape for the driver's cab.

Oval shape

Draw two long metal strips for tracks with planks crossing under them.

Connecting rods

Wheels with thick spokes

Use your finger to smudge the charcoal in a curve around the cylinder shape.

Train shape

Smoke and soot

This steam train is drawn in charcoal and chalk for a sooty, smoky look. You can get this effect by following the steps below.

1 Start your picture by sketching the basic train shape with a thin charcoal line. You can copy the shape from the box on the left.

2 Using charcoal, colour the body a light grey and make the shadowy parts darker. Use white chalk to highlight the very shiny parts.

3 Colour in the smoke with chalk and charcoal. Use your finger to smudge them together in circles to get a dramatic billowing effect.*

*You need to fix a charcoal or chalk picture to stop the colour rubbing off (see page 133).

High-speed models

Modern trains are long and streamlined and sometimes have pointed fronts. You don't need to draw wheels on them. A dark shadow under the body gives a good impression of speed.

Blurred background

Horizontal lines show speed.

Parts of an object look smaller the further away they are. This is called perspective. A train speeding forwards looks big at the front, and narrows to a point, called the vanishing point, at the back.

The vanishing point, where the top and bottom of the train seem to meet.

SOUTHERN PACIFIC

Make wheels, windows and doors smaller the further away they are.

Trains with brains

You can draw train cartoons by exaggerating the way the trains move, and by giving them human faces. Below are some suggestions.

Lines to show braking.

Smoke going the wrong way.

Lines slanted forwards.

This steam train is dragging a heavy load uphill. Its face looks strained and it is puffing out lots of steam.

This high-speed streamlined train is hurtling downhill. It has a happy face. Draw lots of lines around it to give the idea of speed.

This train is braking hard to avoid a tree on the track. It looks surprised and is squashing itself up and leaning backwards.

Planes

Planes can make spectacular pictures because of their sleek, streamlined shapes. You need to make the surface look shiny on the smooth wings and body.

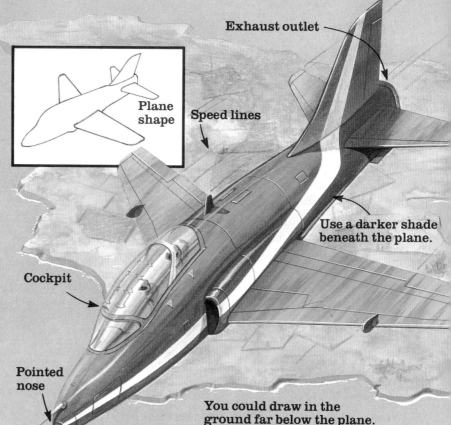

Plane shape

Exhaust outlet

Speed lines

Cockpit

Use a darker shade beneath the plane.

Pointed nose

You could draw in the ground far below the plane.

Jet plane

1 To draw a jet plane, like the Hawk shown here, start with the long, thin shape, shown in red in the box on the right. Then add wings, shown in blue, and a tailplane, shown in green.

2 Paint or colour the body to give a smooth surface, and add pale highlights to make it look shiny.

Take-off

Follow these three steps to draw a picture of a plane taking off above you.

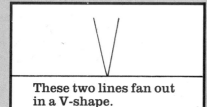

These two lines fan out in a V-shape.

Add building shapes along the horizon.

1 Draw a horizon line across the paper. In faint pencil draw two straight lines fanning out from the centre of the horizon line. Use a ruler to help you get an accurate shape.

2 Draw the plane as shown above, using the lines fanning outwards as the sides of the plane body. Colour it in, adding silhouettes of the airport on the horizon.

3 Draw lines fanning out towards you, for the runway. Add white star shapes along each of the lines to show the runway lights. Make the stars bigger towards the front.

Formation flying

To draw a formation flying team repeat the plane outline shown in the box on the right several times, in any flying pattern you like. You could draw your picture on a bright blue background with trails of different coloured smoke behind the planes.

Draw smoke trails with a series of curves, like this.

Use one bright team colour for the plane shapes.

Plane shape

Sky writer

This cartoon sky-writing plane has a round body and a fat tail and wings. Add a cheerful face and a black nose. Make its smoke trail spell a word or show a pattern of curls and twists.

Bi-plane

Start this picture of a bi-plane by drawing a triangular nose. Then add the wings, with struts and pieces of wire criss-crossed between them. Add the wheels, which are joined

together by another strut. Add two tail pieces sticking out from behind the nose, and a pilot sitting on top. Draw two lines forming loops to show the path made by the plane's exhaust trail.

Turn your plane upside down to make it look like an aerobatic stunt.

Draw in a bird to show the right way up.

119

Bicycles and motorbikes

Bicycle shapes are quite complicated so it is a good idea to do a pencil sketch of your drawing first. Once you have got the shape right you can colour it in.

On these pages you can see how to draw action-packed pictures of bicycles and motorbikes and how to give them a professional finish.

Drawing a bicycle

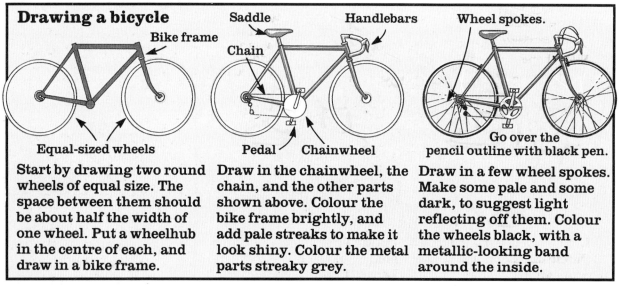

Saddle

Bike frame

Chain

Handlebars

Wheel spokes.

Equal-sized wheels

Pedal   Chainwheel

Go over the pencil outline with black pen.

Start by drawing two round wheels of equal size. The space between them should be about half the width of one wheel. Put a wheelhub in the centre of each, and draw in a bike frame.

Draw in the chainwheel, the chain, and the other parts shown above. Colour the bike frame brightly, and add pale streaks to make it look shiny. Colour the metal parts streaky grey.

Draw in a few wheel spokes. Make some pale and some dark, to suggest light reflecting off them. Colour the wheels black, with a metallic-looking band around the inside.

People on bikes

Here are some pictures of people riding bikes. The stick figures drawn in red are to help you draw the people in the right position. Do the stick figures in light pencil and then gradually build up the body shapes around them.

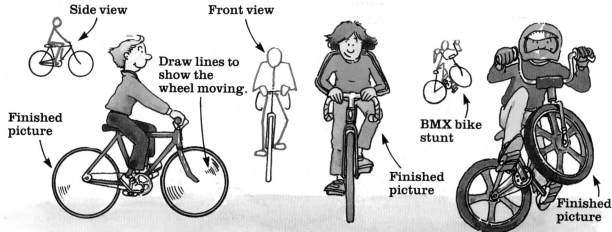

Side view

Draw lines to show the wheel moving.

Front view

Finished picture

BMX bike stunt

Finished picture

Finished picture

Motorbikes

To do a picture of a shiny, streamlined motorbike follow the three steps here.

1 Use the grid method on pages 106-107 to copy the motorbike's main shapes.

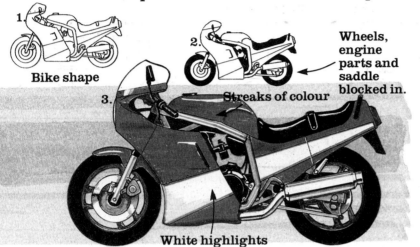

1. Bike shape

2.

Wheels, engine parts and saddle blocked in.

3. Streaks of colour

White highlights

2 Block in the dark areas with one dark colour.
3 You can make the paintwork look shiny by shading it in streaks, using felt tip pens in three or four shades of the same colour. Leave the shiniest part of the body white, or paint on white highlights.

Super-shine

For a super-shiny look draw a motorbike outline in white pencil crayon on black paper. Shade in the shiniest parts and leave the rest of the bike black.

Fun bikes

Lines to show shaking.

This cartoon bike is being ridden over rough ground. It is drawn with a wiggly outline.

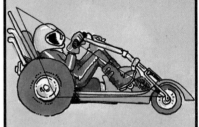

Start this dragster with a triangle shape. The rider has to lean back a long way in the seat.

Speed lines

The basic shape of a rider seen from behind is similar to the front view shown on page 120.

Robots

You can have fun drawing robots because they can be any shape, size or colour you like. Below are some ideas for robot pictures to start you off.

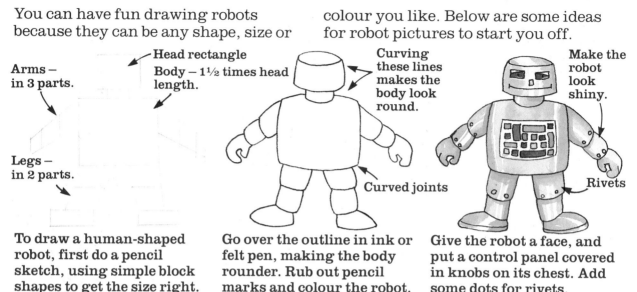

Arms – in 3 parts.

Legs – in 2 parts.

Head rectangle
Body – 1½ times head length.

Curving these lines makes the body look round.

Curved joints

Make the robot look shiny.

Rivets

To draw a human-shaped robot, first do a pencil sketch, using simple block shapes to get the size right.

Go over the outline in ink or felt pen, making the body rounder. Rub out pencil marks and colour the robot.

Give the robot a face, and put a control panel covered in knobs on its chest. Add some dots for rivets.

Robot assortment

You can use all kinds of shapes to draw robots. Below is an assortment of heads, bodies and legs. You could copy or trace these parts, and mix and match them to make up your own robot. Use bright colours and any other extras you like.

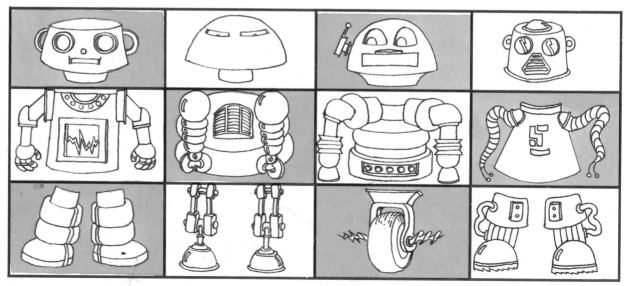

Special robots

Drawing this robot from below makes it look bigger and fiercer. The body gets narrower as it gets further away.

You could try designing a robot to do a special job. This robot has nine arms so it can do lots of household chores at once.

This robot has gone wrong. Its arms and legs are out of control, and there are electric sparks coming out of its control panel.

Hooked hands

Draw big feet.

Crazy eyes

Zigzags and stars to show electric sparks.

Robots you know

Here you can see how to make some of the people and animals you know look like robots. Give them robot bodies but add features so they can be recognized.

Granny robot

Teacher robot

Cat robot

Dog robot

123

Space machines

On the next four pages there are lots of space machine drawings for you to try, using wax and pencil crayons, paints or felt tips.

Shuttle launch

To draw this dramatic space shuttle launch follow the steps below.

1 Draw the launch in three stages, copying the outline on the right. Do the plane-shaped part first, then the fuel tank, then the two rocket boosters.

2 Crayon or paint the shuttle. Streak the colours or add white highlights to make it look shiny.

3 Colour in a cloud of exhaust all around the shuttle, using white, yellow, orange, red and grey.

Fuel tank

Rocket boosters

Plane-shaped shuttle

Cone-shaped engines

Out in space

You could try drawing rockets and planets on white paper, using brightly coloured wax crayon. Then wash over the whole picture with black paint*.

When it is dry, you can add bright stars. Dip an old toothbrush in white paint. Hold it bristles-down over the paper and run your finger towards you along the bristles.

*Tape the picture down on a flat surface while the paint dries, to stop it crinkling.

On the Moon

Here you can see how to draw a picture of the Apollo 11 Lunar Module, the first spacecraft to put a man on the Moon.

1 Use the grid method on pages 106-107 to copy the outline shown in red below.

Module shape

This Lunar Module landed on the Moon on 20 July 1969.

2 Paint the bottom section to look like reflective gold foil, by splodging on yellow, orange and white watercolour paint, so that the colours run together.

3 Paint the top section grey, with shiny-looking white parts and dark shadowy lines to suggest equipment shapes. Paint in the legs and the ladder.

4 Paint the moonscape in shades of grey, with crater shapes. You could add footprints coming from the craft. Paint the sky black, with stars.

Space station

To draw this space station start with the outline below.

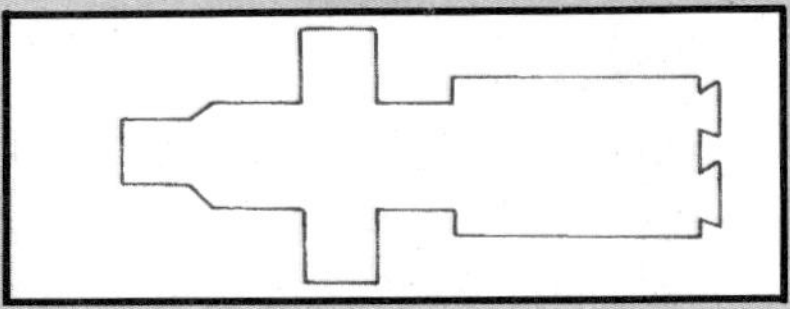

Colour in the space station, and add the parts labelled.

To draw the spacewalking astronaut, start with lots of circle shapes, as shown on the right. Then draw a body outline round the circles.

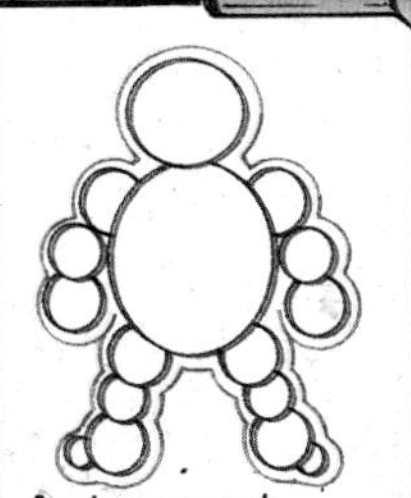

Solar panels

Antenna

Antenna

Engines

Safety line for astronaut

Astronaut shape

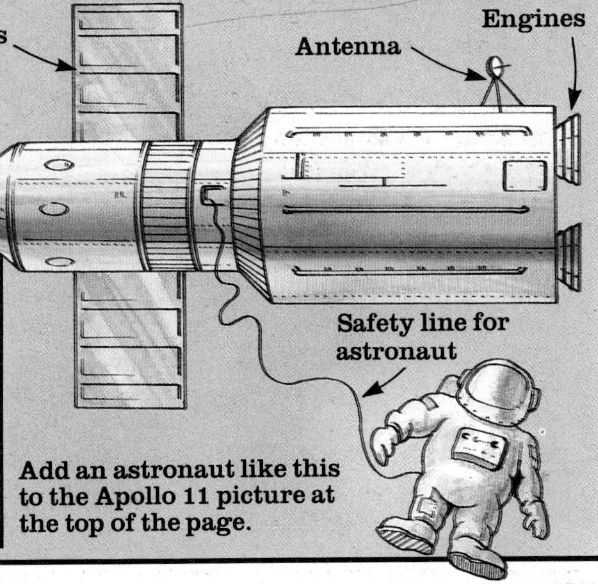

Add an astronaut like this to the Apollo 11 picture at the top of the page.

125

Alien spaceships

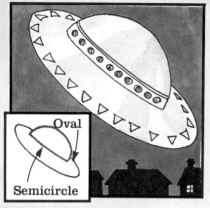

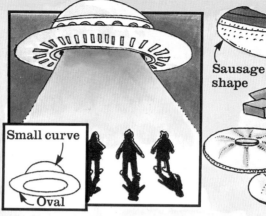

This flying saucer has arrived over Earth. Its shape is made up of part of a circle and part of an oval. Add round windows, triangular lights, and a row of houses below.

This flying saucer is taking off from Earth after a visit. Draw an oval, with a small curve on top to show the roof. Add coloured rays coming out from the bottom of the saucer.

Alien spaceships do not have to be saucer-shaped. You can use any shape you like, and add extras to it such as windows and flashing lights. There are some suggestions above.

Sausage shape

Box shape

Disc shape

Space city

The shapes of the space machines in this science-fiction city are shown in the box on the opposite page. You could copy them and colour them any way you like. Build up a space scene with futuristic plants and houses in the background.

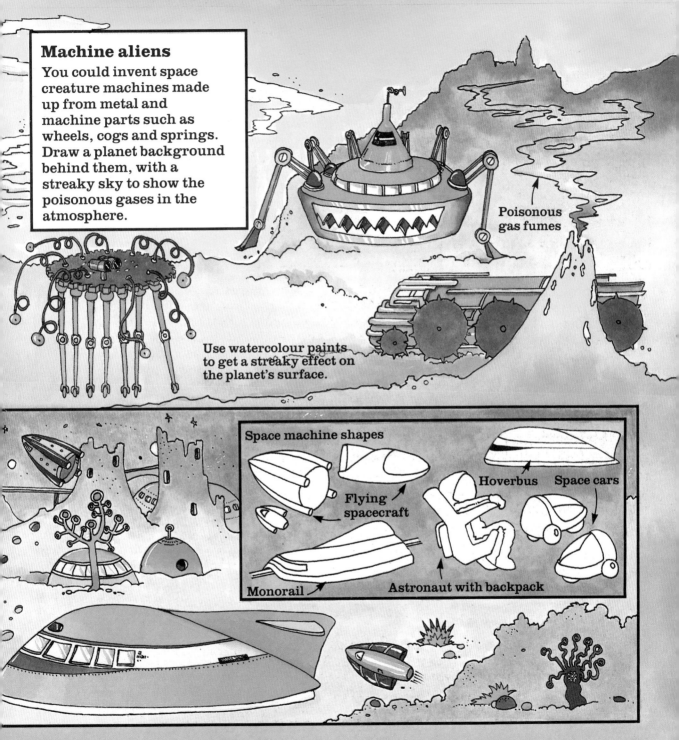

Machine aliens

You could invent space creature machines made up from metal and machine parts such as wheels, cogs and springs. Draw a planet background behind them, with a streaky sky to show the poisonous gases in the atmosphere.

Poisonous gas fumes

Use watercolour paints to get a streaky effect on the planet's surface.

Space machine shapes

Flying spacecraft

Hoverbus

Space cars

Monorail

Astronaut with backpack

Batty inventions

Before you draw your own batty invention, first decide what job you want it to do. On these pages are some ideas to start you off, showing you how to make your machines work using parts such as cogs, wheels and rivets.

Heath Robinson

Heath Robinson was a famous illustrator of the 1930s. He was especially well-known for his pictures of amazing inventions. He made them up using lots of objects joined together in unexpected ways. Each invention was designed to do a special job. The picture on the right is a Heath Robinson idea for a potato peeling machine*.

Trying it yourself

You could try drawing your own invention using everyday bits and pieces joined together in original ways.

Draw in arrows and labels to show how the parts fit together.

Blueprint

Blueprints are photographic copies of designs. These may be given to the manufacturers of a machine, to show how all its parts fit together.

To make a drawing look like a blueprint do it as an outline in dark blue pencil crayon, on pale blue paper.

Tea pourer

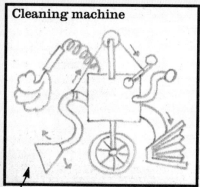

Cleaning machine

Blueprints

*Reproduced by kind permission of The Estate of Mrs J.C. Robinson.

Plant waterer

The plant waterer on the right uses rope, a see-saw, springs, cogs and balls to make the watering can tip over and water the flowers. You could try adapting this idea to make it into a shower spray attached to the bath. There is also an idea for a machine which butters toast on the front cover of this book.

Wind this way.

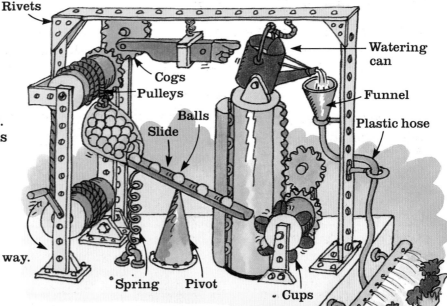

Burglar trap

This idea for a burglar trap is quite simple to draw. It uses wire, weights, shelves and a bucket of water. You could hide the wire among some plants.

When the burglar touches the trip wire, the weight on the top shelf tips on to the lower shelf. This makes the bucket of water fly into the air and land on the burglar.

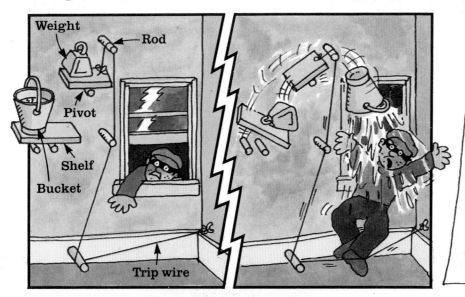

IDEAS LIST

Here are some other suggestions for you to try:

MORNING ALARM
SEED PLANTER
SHOWER SPRAY
PET FEEDER

Drawing from life

To do an accurate drawing of a machine that is in front of you, look at it carefully. Note how wide it is compared to how high it is, and how its different parts compare to each other in size. These sizes are called proportions.

Check the proportions by using your thumb and a pencil as shown below.

1 With one eye closed, hold a pencil out at arm's length. Line up the pencil with one of the edges on the object.

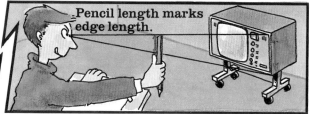

2 Mark the length of the edge, by positioning your thumb at the bottom, and the pencil end at the top.

3 Keeping your thumb in the same position, check how many times this length fits into other parts of the object.

4 Check that the proportions in your drawing compare to each other in a similar way. If they do not, alter your sketch.

Shadows

To get the shadows in the right place on a realistic picture, first see which direction the light is coming from. Then put shadows on areas that are hidden from the light.

Don't forget to show background shadows around any objects you draw. This makes a picture look more realistic*.

Light coming from this way.

Shadow thrown on a table.

These parts are hidden from the light.

130 *Different sorts of shading are shown on

Designing real machines

Engineering designers sketch out their ideas on paper, to help them decide how to build a machine and what it should look like. They try out many ideas before deciding on the best one. On the next few pages there are tips on how they develop a new product, and how you can design your own machine.

Design steps

Here you can see how a designer might develop an idea for a new-style kettle. Follow the three steps below to draw up your own idea for a machine which would be useful. Bear in mind the checklist on the right.

2 Draw this shape bigger ▶ and work out how the different parts will fit together.

◀ 1 Sketch out different shapes and choose the best one.

Designer's checklist

Ask yourself these questions before you design your machine.

What do you want it to do?

How can you make it work efficiently?

How can you make it safe?

How can you make it easy to use?

How can you make it look attractive?

House improvements

You could try to redesign some of the machines in your house, thinking of ways to make them more efficient, practical or attractive. Here are some ideas.

New stereo system with TV incorporated

New toaster design

New-style telephone

New-style deckchair

3 Finish off your ▶ picture by colouring it in, to make it look more attractive. Rub out any pencil lines that are still showing at the end. Label the different parts of the machine clearly.

Wide spout for easy pouring.

Hinged top for easy filling.

Wide, stable base.

Strong handle

131

Computer graphics

Engineers sometimes use computers to help them design machines. This process is called CAD (computer-aided design). They work out measurements which they feed into the computer, so that it produces a simple line drawing of a machine structure.

You can do a picture that looks like a computer design. Draw a machine shape in brightly-coloured lines on a paler background. This computer graphics space shuttle is done with fine felt tips on coloured paper.

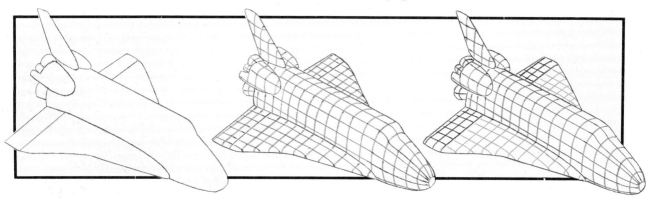

1 Draw the outline of the body in a bright colour.

2 Draw in lines following the contours of the body.

You could use different colours for different parts.

Blow-ups

Designers often use a "blow-up" technique to enlarge one part of a machine and show it in detail.

1 To do a blow-up, draw the whole machine first. Don't colour it in yet.

2 Draw two lines coming from the part you want to enlarge, and a big circle or square.

3 Draw the part bigger and in more detail inside the circle, then colour the whole picture.

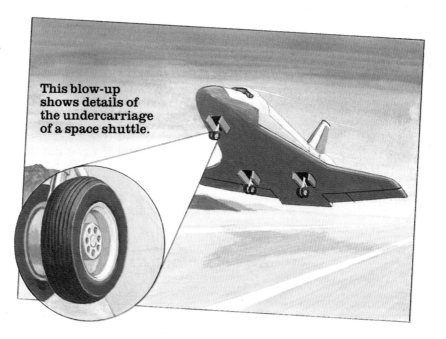

This blow-up shows details of the undercarriage of a space shuttle.

Exploded drawing

This futuristic car design is done as an exploded drawing. The technique is used by designers to show where the different parts of a machine fit, by drawing them hovering near their true position. Follow the steps below to do the picture.

1 To draw the car body shape, shown below, start with the blue lines.

Arrows show where parts are supposed to fit.

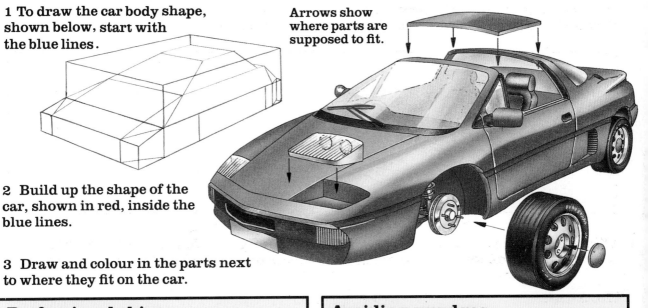

2 Build up the shape of the car, shown in red, inside the blue lines.

3 Draw and colour in the parts next to where they fit on the car.

Professional shine

Artists sometimes use an airbrush to get a smooth effect on machine pictures. This is a device for spraying paint or ink out of a fine nozzle. Before spraying one part of the picture all the rest is protected with a "mask" made from card or masking film. The car drawing above is airbrushed.

Airbrush

mask

Avoiding smudges

Charcoal, chalk and soft pencil smudge easily. You can stop this by spraying a fixative over your finished picture. Art shops sell fixative spray in aerosol cans. It is dangerous to breathe it in so always use it in a well-ventilated area. It should never be used near a flame.

Cutaway pictures

In cutaway pictures, part of a machine's outer casing is cut away to show the inside. This style can give a clear idea of how a machine works.

On these pages you can find out how to draw cutaways of real machines, and there are some ideas for making up your own imaginary cutaways.

Step-by-step cutaway

Here you can see how to draw a cutaway of a bicycle light. To copy machine workings accurately, you need to see them. Bicycle lights are quite easy to take apart safely.*

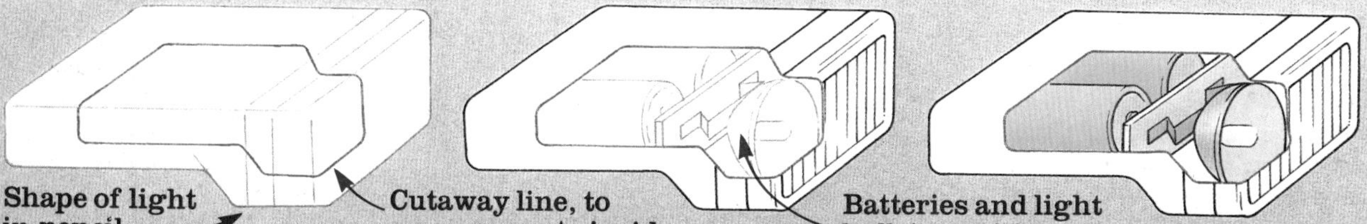

Shape of light in pencil.

Cutaway line, to uncover parts inside.

Batteries and light bulb in position.

1 Pencil in the outer shape of the machine. Draw a line to show the edge of the section that you want to cut away.

2 Draw the machine parts inside the section you have cut away. Go around the parts and the body outline with felt pen or ink.

3 You could colour in the machine parts, but leave the outer shell black and white, as shown above. Rub out any pencil marks.

Car cutaway

You can do this picture by looking under a car bonnet or at a car manual.

1 Draw the car shape (see page 108).

2 Draw a cutaway line round a section of the bonnet, and draw the machinery inside.

3 To show the difference between the inside and outside you could colour in the car body, and simply outline the parts.

You can simplify the shapes of the machine parts.

Leave part of the bonnet on.

*Always take machines apart carefully. Make sure you do not cancel any guarantee by dismantling parts.

Made-up cutaways

You could try drawing a machine cutaway and making up the insides yourself. The parts you draw don't have to be realistic. There are some examples to try below.

Robot

Try doing a robot cutaway. Use the shape on page 122. Then cut away part of the robot's body to show the inner workings. This robot has cogs, wheels and wires inside its control panel. You could also draw a scientist adjusting them.

Telephone

There are tiny people inside this cutaway of a telephone. One is listening to the incoming call, one is taking the message down, and one is shouting it out through the earpiece. Try making up cutaway pictures of machines around your home, showing people busy working inside them.

Big machines

Big machines make good cutaways. Try drawing an aeroplane, a train, or a space station like the one below (see page 125 for the shape). Cut away part of the body to show the people and equipment inside.

People shapes

To draw cartoon people to go inside a machine, follow the steps below.

1 Start with a body and head shape.

2 Add arms, legs, hands and feet.

3 Add details, like clothes and a face.

1.

2.

3.

Index

First published in 1988 by Usborne Publishing Ltd,
Usborne House, 83-85 Saffron Hill, London EC1N 8RT,
England.

Copyright © Usborne Publishing Ltd, 1988

The name Usborne and the device 🐝 are Trade Marks of
Usborne Publishing Ltd.